Joyful Trouble

Based on the True Story of a Dog Enlisted in the Royal Navy

~Large Print Edition~

Patricia C Furstenberg

Print Edition ISBN-13: 9781549636028

Version: 2019-03-22

Cover design: The Book Khaleesi

www.thebookkhaleesi.com

Author's website: www.alluringcreations.co.za/wp

Connect on Twitter: @PatFurstenberg

More books by Patricia Furstenberg:

Puppy, 12 Months of Rhymes and Smiles (also in **large print**)

As Good as Gold (also in **large print**)

Happy Friends (also in **large print**)

The Cheetah and the Dog

The Lion and the Dog

The Elephant and the Sheep

Belle Cat, whiskers on my mat

Huberta the Hippo: Amazing Adventures of a Happy River Horse

Vonk the Horse: Spark, the Bravest Stallion of the 18th Century

Jock of the Bushveld: Africa's Best Loved Dog Hero

Christmas Haiku

Dedication

For my parents,

now wonderful grandparents

Acknowledgments

I would like to thank my amazing husband Gert for always supporting me and believing in me. This book and the amazing experience that came with writing it would not have been possible without his help.

My thanks also go to my extraordinary children, for inspiring me and quietly and lovingly supporting me.

"I'll give you a theory: Man's closest relative is not the chimpanzee, as the TV people believe, but is, in fact, the dog."

Garth Stein, The Art of Racing in the Rain

Contents

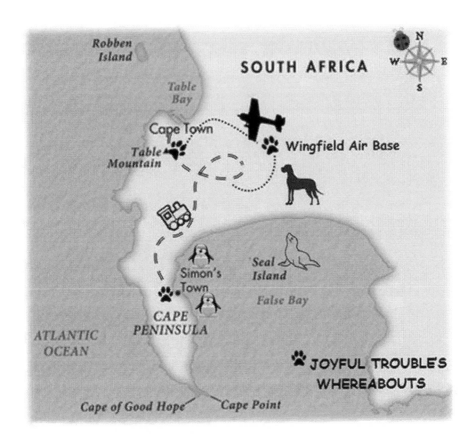

On this map you can follow Joyful Trouble and his many adventures along the Cape Peninsula, the strip of land found at the very tip of South Africa.

Chapter 1

The Dog Parade

'Chase you to the dogs, Tommy!' shouted Ana, rushing ahead.

'Doggies, doggies! Where do they come from, Grandad? Doggies! I have been waiting my whole life to see them, since yesterday! Come on, Grandad,' the little boy trailed behind her, red in the face.

He was clutching his own stuffed dog by the tail, his eyes intent on his sister.

The sailor hat on his head suddenly flew away, looking like a gannet chick on its first voyage. The boy pretended not to notice it, too happy to be without. And what is a lost hat anyway when you have been waiting for the Dog Parade all your life?

Ana slowed down her pace, knowing her little brother would not catch up with her otherwise. He was almost five; she was nine. They would often race but she would always wait for him. Like now.

Using her hand to shield her eyes from the sun she remembered her mother doing the same, one day when they were by the end of the winding road leading to their cottage, waiting for dad to return from his weekly trips. None of them liked being without him. Tommy would say he wished each day was weekend and mom would smile and look away, shading her eyes with her hand. Ana felt big whenever she could do something the same way as her mother.

Her brother ran towards her with the full strength of a little boy. His hair was wild now, ruffled by the wind. Grandma wouldn't like it. They must always wear hats in the sun.

Ana liked to take care ok after her little brother.

'Don't stop, Ana!' he called, panting like a little engine. 'What if we are late? Gosh, we should have started running earlier. We should have started running this morning.'

Luckily Grandad caught up, strolling behind. He stopped by the fallen hat and

3

sighed, bending slowly and painfully to pick it up. He shook off the dust and put it on his own head.

Tommy was still busy running, looking at his feet. He had new shoes and they were too big to allow for growth and toe wiggle. So now he was watching his feet, believing that this prevented him from tripping and falling. That's why he hasn't noticed his sister had stopped.

'Bump!' He ran into her head first.

'Ouch!' she screamed and lost her balance.

'Oops-a-daisy, Ana,' Tommy laughed holding onto her arms to keep his balance. His hands felt hot. The girl smiled and kissed the top of his head. It was steamy and smelled sweet.

Grandad's shadow cast over them.

'Grandad is a sailor!' exclaimed Tommy and patted his own head then pulled Ana's arm.

The noise on the street grew louder. There was life music playing and people were cheering and clapping.

'Doggies! Come, Ana,' Tommy pulled her dress impatiently, 'I want to see the custard Danish!' And just as sudden the boy let go of the dress and was about to run ahead when Grandad grabbed hold of his shirt collar.

The little boy waved his arms and stomped his feet, 'clip-clop', trying to break free. 'Clip-clop, cli-clop' marched the band in rhythm. He knew what would happen next. The hat would get placed back on his head and he did not like it; it was making him hot.

The old man's voice was grave, yet gentle.

'Great Danes, Tommy. They are Great Danes.'

Tommy looked down at his own toy

dog repeating ever so softly, 'great 'anes, great 'anes.' Then, bending his head backwards at a dangerous angle he looked up and said, louder, 'Can you unground me Grandad? Pleeeeze?' Just as Ana began skipping again, pulling at the old man's jacket in turn.

'Come on, Grandad, hurry up! They're here!'

Tommy swiftly grabbed the old man's hand.

'Doggies, doggies! Big doggies!'

The clamour and clatter on the street grew even louder as people were now cheering. The town brass band came in sight, playing a joyful tune, leading the parade, with the drum major displaying his overly ornate uniform and swinging his golden ceremonial mace in rhythm. Ana thought he looked as proud as a peacock.

Everyone knew the dog procession will soon show up.

A gust of wind playfully pulled at the girl's blue and white dress. For a short moment the soft material billowed around her like a Royal Navy flag. A few older men smiled, instinctively straightened their shoulders, looking taller and younger.

Then the straw hat slipped backwards, revealing her brown hair and two red cheeks. Grandad prepared to catch that hat too, but the elastic sewed by Grandma held it in place. The old man sighed in relief.

Ana looked up with bright eyes, her demanding, high-pitched voice making itself heard, questioning as usual.

The three of them, Ana, Tommy and Grandad, almost caught up with the crowd by Main Street when the boy looked ahead and froze. He threw up his arms, his eyes policing the road. The dog procession came in view and what a sight that was! Tommy had never seen anything like it.

The old man smiled and picked him up, then spoke. He had to raise his voice to cover the noise made by the other onlookers, yet his voice remained gentle.

'They're not doggies, child. They're big dogs and tall ones too. They're Great Danes.'

'Why are they called that, Grandad?' The girl seemed to suddenly remember something. 'Is that a title? Are they Lords or something?'

Ana grabbed hold of the old man's other hand for support. She jumped, again and again, trying to see past the row of spectators standing alongside the road.

It was April the 1st and the Parade in Honour of Joyful Trouble was about to begin. Each year people and dogs would gather on the Main Street in Simon's Town to celebrate the birth and life of a one-of-a-kind dog and seaman, the only one to be enlisted in the British Royal Navy during World War Two.

There would also be a look-alike

competition and the winner, the dog to resemble Joyful Trouble the most, would lead the parade, dogs, people, brass band and onlookers, all the way to Jubilee Square. This was the place where the brass statue of the real Joyful Trouble, Great Dane and Ordinary Seaman, was found. Joyful Trouble, a friendly and an extraordinary military working dog.

Ana had given up jumping. She was crouching now, trying to catch a glimpse of the parade while peering between the legs of the first row spectators.

Finally, the parade came down the road. The brass band marched ahead, the musicians wearing beautiful uniforms, their instruments polished, shining golden in the sun.

Ana admired the musical instruments. Some were so big, almost as big as her brother; she wondered if they were just as heavy. They certainly didn't look light. Neither did her brother, she couldn't pick him up anymore as though he was made of stones. But he wasn't, she smiled to herself; he was soft and cuddly.

Lost in thought, her eyes dazed by the shining instruments, the girl didn't noticed that now she had a prime spot, right in the front of everyone else.

When something startling happened…

Chapter 2

Tears and handkerchiefs

The first dog showed up.

The brass band had just passed them. There were girls and boys performing in it, tall and short. Ana was still wondering how a woman that small could play an instrument that big, as curled as snail and with an opening a big as Grandma's cooking pot.

Perhaps she too, one day, could play such an instrument.

One funny thought came to her; could the musicians keep snacks inside their instruments? A peanut butter and jam sandwich for Tommy, a slice of banana bread for Grandad? An ice cream - no, that would melt. A toasted cheese and mayo for her. The bigger instruments could certainly hold a few nibbles. But will that muffle the sound? The little girl wanted to ask Grandad when… she found herself standing right in front of the first dog.

Now ahead of everyone else in the crowd the girl had stepped forward, almost to the middle of the road, while looking after the brass band. And, with the musicians gone, the dogs and their owners were now coming down the road. One by one. And the first dog was standing right in front of her.

15

Ana's mouth fell open but no noise came out. Her eyebrows rose and her eyes crossed. Her face changed colour from red to very red, all over.

Ana's own small nose was now level with the muzzle of a very tall, brown, four-legged creature. Two big, calm hazel eyes measured the small girl from underneath a pair of soft eyebrows. A warm and moist breath, smelling of grass and something else altogether, fell onto the girl's face. The dog calmly sniffed her cheek while Ana shut her mouth tight, holding her breath, only her eyes growing bigger.

A gentle tug on the leash and the dog stepped aside and away, moving on. His tail swished a bit and its tip touched the girl's arm. The big dog was now marching down the road, its tall legs stepping slowly, graciously carrying its big body, his long tail lazily hanging low.

Grandad's reassuring arm stretched right on time, pulling the little girl from the middle of the street.

Ana's high-pitched cry got lost in the general disorder. People were applauding, dogs were barking, and the town's brass band was now ringing further and further to another joyful tune. And nobody seemed to notice the wind, trying to blow their music sheets away.

Only the Grandad standing behind noticed the fear in the girl's voice.

'Great 'ane shook your hand, Ana!' exclaimed Tommy, wiggling to get down. As soon as his feet touched the ground the boy grabbed his sister's arm. Studying it, checking for any marks.

'Great 'ane said HELLO!'

Grandad groaned as he put one knee to the ground. He pulled the girl close to his chest. Ana threw her arms around his

18

neck.

Not knowing what else to do, Tommy threw his small arms around his sister and his grandfather.

The girl was quiet now. From her Grandfather's arms she watched as the parade disappeared out of sight.

Tommy patted her arm again.

'Great 'ane said hello, Ana,' he repeated softly.

'I guess so,' smiled Grandad encouragingly.

Ana looked Grandad in the eyes.

'They are so BIG, Grandad,' she whispered.

'That's why they're called great my child,' replied the old man while removing a handkerchief from his jacket's breast

19

pocket.

'They're still dogs, only big,' and saying so he wiped the girl's eyes, then helped her clean her nose.

Tommy wiped his eyes with the sleeve of his shirt, just in case, and pulled his nose in.

'It sniffed my cheek,' whispered Ana and without noticing she squeezed the old man's hair with one hand while gingerly touching her face with the other, making sure it was still there.

At this, Tommy came closer and promptly sniffed his sister's face. His nose wrinkled.

'Sausage,' he declared, pushing his own toy dog towards his sister's face. 'Smell,' he said.

With a gentle hand Ana pushed the toy away.

Grandad smiled, although the girl's other hand was still firmly tucked into his hair.

'He was curious. He wanted to know what you ate for breakfast. A dog's nose, or his muzzle, is one of the most sensitive areas for touch on a dog.'

'His nose was wet, Grandad,' whispered Ana and tears welled in her eyes.

'Do you know why? There is a beautiful story about it. It happened on Noah's Arch. It is said that Noah had two dogs on his Arch and they were responsible with safety on board. One day, while patrolling, the dogs discovered a little leak in the Arch's hull. Working as a team, one dog ran for help, while the other dog used his nose to plug the hole and keep everyone safe. And that's why dogs' noses are wet, to remind us of their fidelity and courage. '

Tommy touched his nose thoughtfully. Grandad smiled.

'Or perhaps he sniffed you because he wanted to make friends. Great Danes are very friendly dogs,' said the old man. 'They love being among people. They are affectionate and gentle, despite their big size.'

'Huuuuge!' exclaimed Tommy and he even managed to whistle, which made Ana laugh. The little boy beamed and tried to whistle again.

The girl's hand squeezing in Grandad's hair loosened its grip and he

23

Patricia Furstenberg

sighed in relief.'

'But I don't like smelling people, Grandad. I shake hands,' said Ana finding her voice again.

'A dogs' brain is much more interested in smell than the human brain is. So much so that there is an area in their brain that is four times bigger than that in the human brain - dedicated just to smells! In fact, a dog's nose is over 1000 times more sensitive than that of a human's. And dogs can smell each and every scent that makes up an odour. For example, when you smell Grandma's tasty chicken masala, a dog would smell chicken, tomatoes, potatoes, parsley, onion, carrot, celery, cumin and every other spice Grandma put inside.'

'His mouth smelled funny, Grandad! He's not brushing his teeth!' said Ana.

Tommy looked down the road, where the parade now disappeared out of view. Then he looked at his own toy dog and smelled it. Nodding approvingly, he hugged his toy.

'Why are they called Great Danes, Grandad?' said the girl.

'Oh, now this is a bit of a story. Many years ago, about 300, at the same time Jan van Riebeeck came to this part of the world with his ship, him being the first settler here, a Dutch, another man was travelling through France. His name was Compte de Buffon...'

Ana burst in laughter. 'Was he a clown, Grandad?'

25

'Not at all. His family owned the village of Buffon so their title had to incorporate its name. It showed their importance. Compte de Buffon was well schooled. He was a naturalist, studying nature and life, a cosmologist, studying the sky and the stars, and a mathematician. He also wrote many, many books and he was a gifted swordsman, something in high demand in those times.'

'I am a swordsman too, Grandad,' exclaimed Tommy pocking around with a stick. Grandad lifted an eyebrow. He was sure that Tommy would be able to find a stick even in the desert.

'Now one day Compte de Buffon was on a nature hike in France when he observed the most unusual animal he had ever seen in his life. Almost as tall as a small horse, yet he was not a pony. As tall as a calf, yet he was not a cow. His croup, the bottom part at the back, was just as tall as the wheel of their carriage. And to top it all the dog showed a friendly and gentle nature. Compte de Buffon was so impressed by this encounter that he labelled the new dog breed 'le Grande Denois' and he told everyone about it. And the name stuck.'

The entire dog parade had passed them by now so the three of them were bringing up the rear, much to Tommy's disappointment.

'I want to see the doggies, come Grandad! Please?'

27

'Great Danes, Tommy,' Anna pointed out.

'Actually, Tommy is not so wrong. In Germany they are called 'Deutsche doggen'.

'So where do Great Danes come from, Grandad?'

'They come from up the road, Ana,' said Tommy and his eyebrows went up, up with his hand that pointed towards the top of the hill. 'From there. They came from there.'

Grandad laughed and Ana smiled and waved her head in defeat, remembering her mom doing just so.

'Great Danes come from long ago, a long, long time ago. Egyptian monuments had murals depicting such dogs. Romans

28

probably brought them to Europe where they were used in hunting - since they were so majestic and so strong. And they used them as guard dogs too. But with the passing of time and a change in human's interests and activities the Great Dane breed also changed, becoming gentler and more suited for company. So much so that people even tried to involve the Great Danes in the Great War, as MWD, Military Working Dogs or as mere mascots - both just as valuable.'

That night at bedtime, two heads neatly brushed and two faces scrubbed twice were peering from underneath their duvets. And a little girl with bright eyes, not looking in the least sleepy, and a little boy hugging a toy dog, both asked for the

29

story of Joyful Trouble.

'Tell us the story of Joyful Trouble the Great Dane, Grandad. Please,' smiled Ana sweetly.

It always worked.

'Great 'ane story, Gran'ad,' yawned Tommy then added 'wrap me like a chicken wrap, Grandad.' And after a break, 'please and thank you.'

Chapter 3

Someone sits at the Commander's desk

'Well,' said Grandad as he leaned forward.

Ana and Tommy stretched their necks on the pillow. Grandad always told beautiful stories. And this was a real one!

The old man smiled, his eyes cast far away to a blue sky and the call of seagulls across a sea of turquoise and foam. It smelled of salt and of wet wood and his own footsteps, faster and lighter, were echoing along the ship's plank.

31

There was excitement in the air. Life was good and it laid ahead of him, as exciting and inviting as a sea voyage.

'Well, since this is a yarn and sea story, a sailor story and sailors are famous for spinning tales, for telling sea stories that may not be entirely truth, I'll begin with the traditional opening 'this is not so…' he started and his eyes rested on the seaman hat he had placed on his knees.

'But all is true.

'The year was 1939 and I had just joined the Royal Navy at the British naval garrison in Cape Town, South Africa. It was a big thing for a young man those days. And although I was only an Ordinary Seaman, I was very proud of my bell bottomed trousers, white shirt and flat bottomed blue hat,' and saying this he gently laid the sailor hat onto the girl's head.

'Am I a sailor now, Grandad?' giggled the girl.

'A seaman,' said Tommy. 'Anybody is sailor. Seaman has THAT hat,' he said and pointed towards Ana's head. Then he looked at the old man for approval. 'Right so, Grandad?'

'Right so, Tommy.'

The hat was too big for her child's head and it soon slipped forward, hiding her face altogether.

Grandad laughed and, narrowing his eyes, he rearranged the hat. Soon the pair of bright eyes he cherished so much smiled at him again.

'Story, Grandad,' said Tommy

'It was hard work being a seaman.

And we had to work all day long. We had

to carry goods onto the ship. We had to bring the food supplies onto the ship, drinking water too and make sure it was enough for everybody and plenty left for cooking. We had to clean the ship and keep it tidy at all times. And some of us even had to cook for all the others! And I was very serious about my work. Because only the hardworking seamen were being given duties...'

'You wanted duties, Grandad?' asked Ana.

'Duties to play with?' asked Tommy.

'No, silly,' said Ana. 'Duties are chores. Like when you have to...' and the girl frowned, thinking of an example, 'like when you have to pick up your toys.'

Tommy's eyes went wide open.

'You wanted to clean, Grandad?'

The old man laughed.

'Sometimes, Tommy, it is nice to have to do something. Because it can be something that you enjoy doing and it also gives you a sense of accomplishment.'

'Like taking care of dogs?' said Ana.

'Yes, like taking care of dogs, but no ordinary dogs.'

Tommy pulled his toy dog closer and kissed it.

'I take care of you,' he whispered.

The old man relaxed in his chair, stretched out his legs, smiling at the two children. The girl's eyes, peering from underneath the seaman's cap, were filled with curiosity and excitement. The boy's

36

eyes were lovingly watching his own toy dog. The toy was bouncing up and down, pouncing on the duvet.

'Woof, woof,' said the boy.

When the room was quiet again the old man went on with his story.

'We were not at sea those days, although there was serious talk of another big war in Europe.

'Our ship was anchored in the harbour, ready to leave on a short notice. The harbour was named Simon's Bay, but sailors mostly used its old name, False Bay, that was given by navigators hundreds of years ago because it was often confused with Table Bay, a dangerous bay found a little further to the north.

'The beautiful town of Simon's Town began to develop in the 1600s when the Dutch navigators first stopped here in search for fresh water, fruits and vegetables. About the same time Compte de Buffon had first spotted the great danes. Sea navigators liked this place, with its surrounding mountains and safe, protected bay. At first Simon's Town had only a small military base, a baker who produced the bread, a carpenter who helped with wood needed for shelters and ships, a blacksmith who produced tools and horse shoes and a slaughter house, for meat. But much later, during our times in World War Two, the Simon's Town dock yard had repaired hundreds of warships and merchant vessels and, most importantly, was the home of the Royal Navy's South Atlantic Fleet.

'Now, when we, sailors, were done with our chores and nothing urgent was in sight we would get our free time.'

'Morsel,' said Tommy half asleep, 'a morsel would be nice, Gran'ad. Can I have a Twik?'

'You mean Twix,' said Ana.

'No, I only want one,' said Tommy from his dream.

Grandad smiled and went on.

'Then one morning our Commander-in-Chief called me into his office. This had never happened before. I was an Ordinary Seaman. A Commander would not call an Ordinary Seaman into his office. The most he would do is pass on an order to him.

'But I knew I did nothing wrong so I went in with a happy heart. I was hoping he would give me a task. I didn't look into the matter too deeply. When your superior summons you, you obey and you do so as soon as possible. But if the Commander-in-Chief calls for you, then you obey twice as fast.

'So I made sure I had my clean uniform on, my hat positioned just right, and my shoes polished.'

'Did you knock first, Grandad?' asked Ana, frowning a little. She was just learning that one must knock before entering someone else's room, a task Tommy was still struggling with. He would first enter, then knock, at best.

'Of course I did,' said the old man. 'Entering a superior's office without knocking is a serious offence in the navy.'

Tommy opened one eye.

'One can get in big trouble,' explained Grandad. So I knocked and waited to be invited inside. And my hand shook a bit as I grabbed the door knob. Then I took a deep breath and open the door. I don't

41

know what I was expecting, perhaps a big room, given that he was the superior officer. The Commander's office was only a tad bigger than any other room on the ship. It had a large desk facing the door with a chair behind it, a bookcase on the side, filled all the way to the top and a very soft carpet. I still remember this because my feet resonated 'clip-clop' as I approached the door, but as soon as I stepped inside I felt my shoes sinking into the rug, all noise muffled, as soft as a cloud. And that's when I saw it.'

'What did you saw in your Commander's office, Grandad? What was it?' said Ana. She wanted the story started already.

'The question is not WHAT was in my

Commander's office. But WHO was in his office. Who do I see sitting on the Commander's chair? At his desk? Sitting like a man would, with his bottom on the chair and his upper body sticking above the desk… As tall as a man.'

'Who was it, Grandad?' asked Ana in anticipation.

'I stared and I couldn't believe my eyes. And all the time I said to myself: this is not a dream, this is not a dream. For I have heard my Commander's voice from behind the door just seconds before!'

'Who was it, Grandad?' said Ana again, this time propped up on one elbow.

'Who who who,' echoed Tommy,

43

holding his eyes wide open with his fingers and trying his best at imitating an owl.

Chapter 4

Trouble with a capital T

'It was a dog! A really big dog! In fact, it was the biggest dog I had ever known in my life. It was almost, almost as big as a small horse,' and Grandad measured with his hand from the ground.

Ana's eyes grew bigger as she smiled.

'As big as the dog I met at the parade, Grandad?'

'Great 'ane,' added Tommy and he made his toy bounce again.

'Yes,' said the old man, 'as big as that, a Great Dane.'

'So, as I entered my Commander's Office, I noticed the dog. And I looked around for the Commander, but he was nowhere in sight. The office was quiet, some light coming in through a small, round window. And no one else around but me and the huge dog sitting at my Commander's desk.

'I closed the door behind and looked towards the desk again, not sure what to do next. If my Commander would have sat there I would have looked him in the eye and salute. But since a dog was seated, I wasn't sure what to do. The dog's eyes were soft, with no tension in the brows so I looked straight into his eyes and gave my salute.

'Reporting for duty, Sir!'

'And what did the dog say, Grandad?'

giggled Ana with a hand over her mouth.

'The dog said nothing; he just sniffed me over the desk and barked. Just once and not very loud either. But my Commander walked in from the store room just as I saluted the dog.'

'Thinking to change your division, Seaman?' was all he said to me then moved around his desk to be near his chair. At this moment the dog licked the Commander's hand then slowly, but firmly, pushed his head underneath it. And before you knew it, the Commander-in-Chief of the Royal Navy South Atlantic was scratching the dog's head.'

'How did he knew to ask this, the dog? How, Grandad?'

'Dogs lived near humans for

thousands of year, they are very good at reading our body language and at making themselves understood. But only to those who can speak dog.'

'Speak dog?'

'Yes, speak dog. Dogs tell us a lot through the way they move their tail, their ears. You should never rush a dog into a greeting. For example, if a dog's ears are up, but not pushed forward and his tail is low and relaxed the dog is friendly. If his ears are forward and his eyes are wide open, his tail raised, the dog is checking things out. But if you see vertical wrinkles between his eyes, his nose wrinkled and his tail stiff, then you better watch out for that dog and show your respect, keep your distance.'

'Isn't it the same if the hair on his back is raised?'

'You are right, Ana. That dog is fearful and might be aggressive. Shame, something got to him, not necessarily you. Dogs have an amazing memory and smells can often trigger past experiences, good or bad. A dog can often react on instinct. If a dog's tail is down, tugged behind his hind legs, his ears flat back and he barely makes eye contact, that dog is scared and worried and we owe it to him to be gentle and calm.

'Most of all, dogs love human interaction because they are social animals. Just like humans and wolves, dogs live in a pack. Did you know that dogs descend from wolves? Wolves are pack animals, each member of the pack having a specific role. But ever since dogs have been domesticated and began to interact with humans they began counting on us to satisfy this new formed human-canine bond. As they have less pure dog on dog interactions they crave our attention. It helps them remain mentally happy and healthy.

'Pawing is one of the ways dogs let us know about their needs. Dogs are very good at transmitting information to humans, especially if it is for accomplishing a common goal. For example, if a dog brings you one of your shoes it might mean that he wants you to put them on. Because he knows that whenever you put on your shoes you go

51

outside. And at this specific moment your dog needs you to go outside because he need to go out and pee.

Tommy burst into giggles. 'You said the p word, Grandad.'

'Such a clever dog, Grandad,' smiled Ana. 'And what did the Commander do?'

'Nothing; he smiled at the dog and said: 'Such a clever dog, Trouble, you're such a clever dog.'

And Grandad smiled towards the children and the children smiled back; Ana wide awake, Tommy in his sleep.

'And that was the first time I ever saw my Commander smile; but not the last.

'Then the Commander looked at me and said: 'Word goes you're good with animals, especially dogs. Is that so?' And

I said yes, I get along with anybody. 'Have you seen this dog before?' the Commander asked me next.

'Now, some dogs look alike, but some dogs are made to stand out and such a dog was the dog sitting at the Commander's desk. I would have recognized that dog out of a million. He was a very special dog, friendly too. And very, very clever. So I said yes, I had seen the dog before; without giving out too much detail.'

Grandad smiled and stretched out his legs.

'You see, I knew that dog very well, but I was taking my cues from him. If he wasn't giving away our friendship, then I wasn't going to do it either.'

Ana's eyes grew larger and a smile curled the corners of her mouth.

'You are well aware of the situation this dog had caused around Simon's Town, Seaman?' asked the Commander further. Situation, was mild said,' explained Grandad.

'There was big conflict that's been caused by that dog. The seamen and the people loved him, but the officials, well; let's just say they were not very fond of him. So much so that the poor dog was in trouble for being just that, a friendly four legged creature.

'So I said yes, I knew what was at stake.'

'Steak!' exclaimed Tommy suddenly, wide awake. 'I'm hungry!'

54

Grandad laughed softly.

'It's getting late, children. Maybe we should continue the story tomorrow.'

But Tommy was already out of bed and by the door.

'I'm hungry,' he rubbed his tummy.
Then he looked into his toy dog's eyes.
'You hungry?' and without waiting for an
answer he proclaimed, 'we're hungry,'
and opened the door calling out for
Grandma.

'What trouble was the dog in,
Grandad?' said Ana with half a voice, her
eyes pleading.

'Well, child, the railway officials have
warned the dog's owners many times that
they will put the dog to sleep if the
situation is not fixed right away.'

'But what did the dog do?'

'Well, he took day trips by train;
without a ticket!'

Chapter 5

Once there was a puppy

At this, Ana laughed, tears trimming her eyelashes.

'Why would a dog ride by train, Grandad? Where would he go?'

'An ordinary dog, perhaps not; but this special dog liked to ride trains wherever seamen went. You see, he loved all people, but he adored seamen. Wherever the blue bell-bottomed trousers, square blue collars and flat topped caps would go, Trouble would go too.'

'Trouble?' said Ana.

'Trouble,' said Grandad. 'For this was the Great Dane's name. At least the one he was called by; especially by us, his seamen friends.'

'What was his real name?' said Ana.

'Nobody knew his real name, except for his owner, but he was a man very busy with his new job in Simon's Town. You see, when he was a puppy with big paws, proof that he will grow big and tall. A puppy with long, floppy ears and a wide nose and a busy tail, Trouble belonged to a little boy.'

Grandad glanced towards the hallway; noises were coming from the kitchen.

'It is only fair that little puppies belong

to little girls and boys, isn't it?'

'My puppy,' proclaimed Tommy from
the door, swinging his own toy by the tail.

A delightful aroma of cooked
sausages burst into the room.
The small boy came by his

59

grandfather's side just as the bedroom door closed.

'Five more minutes, you three,' Mom's voice resonated from the hallway.

Tommy reached in his pyjama pocket and took out a handful of cookie crumbs.

'For you, Grandad,' he said and he allowed the old man to choose a few crumbs. Then the small hand closed again and the boy moved by the bed. He emptied the rest of the crumbs on the duvet, right in front of his sister's nose.

'For you, Ana. Dinner,' he said, then climbed in. He laid his own toy dog on his chest, but it fell forward.

'I'm not food, doggie. I'm not food,' whispered Tommy then louder, 'Doggie story, Grandad, please?'

The old man smiled and sighed in resignation.

'When Trouble was a puppy,' he began, 'he belonged to a boy. And wherever the boy went, Trouble was sure to follow. And whenever the boy needed help, he always knew he could count on Trouble to support him, help him and guard him.'

'My Trouble,' whispered Tommy to his toy dog, then squeezed him to his chest.

Grandad smiled and Ana smiled too then asked, 'Why do dogs think they have to guard humans?'

'Dogs, much like their ancestors, the wolfs, are programmed. They have it in their blood to guard their own territories. Their extraordinary smell helps them at this, their fantastic hearing and their eyesight too. Although dogs have been living near humans for thousands of years and they depend almost completely on us for food and shelter, I think that to them we are not fitted to protect ourselves against potential intruders. We can't hear the movement that isn't into our earshot, we can't smell dangerous odours, be it human or chemical. And we definitely can't see through walls. Dogs can't see through walls either, but their fine hearing and acute sense of smells makes it look like that. For dogs, the safety of the group is of supreme importance. I think that's why dogs feel the need to protect us.'

'Even a puppy?'

'Even a puppy will protect his human. One day the boy went along the road looking for sticks. He wanted a rather long one to make himself a staff. Trouble followed him.'

Grandad glanced towards his shoes, making a small sideways movement with his right foot.

'The boy enjoyed feeling the dust between his toes and he would kick small dust storms as he would walk along. And Trouble enjoyed being with his boy, although every now and then the dust would make him sneeze. Absorbed how he was by the dust and the toes and the search for sticks, the boy soon got lost. He only realized so when he was too far to see the town, and too close to the

63

forest. So the boy let himself fall on the side of the road, in the dirt, and began to cry. And the tears and the dust soon drew long lines of dirt on the boy's small, pink face. Trouble sat beside him, with his head on the boy's knee. And after the first wave of sadness and despair washed over the boy Trouble nudged him with his nose and the boy hugged the dog, thankful for comfort.'

Tommy held his toy dog close to his chest.

'We are lost, how will we ever get home?' said the boy.

'At the sound of those words the dog jumped to his feet and began pulling at the boy's shirt. And he pulled and he pulled and never let go until the two of them were right in front of the boy's house.

'For the dog, although a puppy, knew the way back home. '

'Really?' Exclaimed Ana. 'How was that possible, he was only a puppy.'

'Dogs have what humans call homing instinct. I think dogs just call it love. They can use their senses to find their way back home or to even track down a beloved human that went away. Either way, it is still a bit of a mystery, like other powers dogs seem to have. Knowing when their owners come home long before they even arrive at the front door, for example. Or knowing when their owners are in danger.

'One year after I enrolled in the Royal

Navy the Germans were bombing many places in Europe, especially in London. Since we had close ties with the British, we heard many war stories.

'One was about an extraordinary dog named Buddy. Buddy's owners were the Evans and they lived in a little house in a quiet neighbourhood of London. Soon after the Second World War started Buddy proved he had extraordinary powers. He knew when an air raid will begin, before it even started, and he will whine and scratch on the front door. This would alert Mr. Evans who would run into the yard with his bugle, Mr. Evans being a musician in a local brass band. He would play the 'Reveille' for the entire neighbourhood, alerting everyone that it is time to run to the air-raid shelter. Now the 'Reveille' is chiefly used in the military to wake the soldiers at sunrise, but since it is high tuned, fast pace it is impossible to miss. I guess Mr. Evans found it best suited for the occasion. Needless to say Buddy never missed an air-raid.'

'He surely had a very good hearing,' smiled Ana.

'You would think. But Buddy was death. He was born like that. How he knew when the air-raid would begin, remains a mystery. What is sure is that he was loved and spoiled by the entire neighbourhood. And the Evans loved him for being himself and brightening their lived during hard times.'

Grandad smiled at the girl's amazed

expression.

'Back to our puppy… The boy's parents were very grateful to see their son back home all in one piece, especially since it was almost dark. They've been so worried, the entire household was up, looking for their little boy.'

'Did they thank the dog, Grandad?'

'Very much so,' winked the old man. 'He got a fresh bone every day for a week.'

'On another occasion,' said the grandfather, 'the boy and his dog went peach picking, for a pie. That's what the boy told his mom and he even had a basket with him. But instead of picking the peaches, the boy ate and ate and ate.

68

The peaches were so big and tasty, sweet and yummy, the boy couldn't stop himself.

'And as he stretched for one more ripe peach, his hands sticky with their juice, he slipped from the tree and fell to

69

the ground. Right beside his dog, who, not liking peaches, was dozing on the ground, in the shade of the tree.'

'Oh, no! The poor, poor boy!' exclaimed Ana. 'Was he hurt?'

'Ouch!' exclaimed Tommy.

'I am afraid so,' sighed Grandad. 'His leg was broken.'

'Did the doggie went home to fetch help?' said Ana full of hope.

'No, he did not,' said Grandad. 'In fact, being a bit older now, taller and stronger, he carried the boy home, on his back.'

'Really? Ana laughed and clapped her hands.

'Horsey, horsey,' whispered Tommy and before he could say 'horsey' one more time, he was fast asleep.

'Yes, just like a horsey, Tommy. Fact is, the dog seemed to always know just what the boy said or needed - and all by looking at him. Dogs do pay attention to our eyes' movement. They look where we look, they notice what we are interested in and they learn to read us; they learn from us. Because they love us and they trust us and all they want to do is to know us and make us happy. The connection between man and dog is a bond forged in trust.'

'Dogs want to make us happy?'

'They do, child, they do. Dogs have our best interests at heart, all the time. That's what motivates them. Much more than getting what they want. You see,

71

dogs are always aware of what is going on around them and they act upon it. I don't mean only aware of who walks into a room, who passes on the street and what meat is cooked in the kitchen. Dog's actions and reactions are a result of our own plus of their own thoughts. Dogs know exactly who we are and they like us just the way we are. Dogs don't expect us to change for them and are very happy just being near us.

'This is what I noticed after spending all that time with Joyful Trouble. Dogs watch us and worry about us, about our safety, especially being the good sniffers and listeners they themselves are.

'Just because we see the dogs running, eating and barking, it does not mean that this is all there is to being a dog. Once you get to know a dog you realise that the whole running, eating and barking has a whole new meaning to you.

'Do you know how humans would call the care Trouble the puppy showed his boy?'

'How?'

'Empathy. It means the ability to understand and share the feelings of another. Trouble the puppy cared for his lost and hurt human friend. He comforted him, kept him safe and brought him home. He didn't left him alone. And he thought of a plan to bring him home when the boy could not walk.'

Ana kept silent for a while, her hands covering her cheeks. Then she smiled happily.

'I like Joyful Trouble, Grandad. I like him a lot. I wish…'

They stood in silence, only Tommy's light snore marking the passing of the time.

'Soon after that summer of fun the school began and the boy had to go to school for a long time. And he couldn't take his dog with him. So his parents promised to take good care of the dog. And so they did, or they tried to. But they didn't know the dog as well as the boy did. To them he was only a dog in need of food, water and shelter. And that's what they offered him while the dog waited. For a long time young Trouble would wake up in the morning and head for the gate through which the boy left. And he would sit there and wait all day long. Sometimes he would lay, sometimes he would move in the shade, but his eyes would never leave the gate. Waiting for his boy. Then something extraordinary happened.'

'The boy returned!' exclaimed Ana and she clapped   her hands in anticipation.

Tommy stirred in his sleep.

'Not quite,' said Grandad. 'One day the dog became restless. He was pacing the yard, whining softly, heading for the gate then returning to the house and for three days he did not eat any food, only had water. And on the fourth day the boy was home.'

'Holiday,' whispered Ana loudly.

'Indeed it was. And young Trouble had known, somehow, that his boy was on his way home.

'That's why, when the family had to change town because of the boy's father's new job, the dog came with them. And that's how Trouble arrived to Simon's Town.'

After saying this grandfather pushed his hands against the armrests of the chair and stood up slowly. He tucked the blanket around the girl and bent over to kiss her hair. The hair was soft and her head was warm, just like a puppy's.

'Grandad, why did Trouble like seamen so much?'

'Oh,' said the old man and scratched

his chin for a minute. It made a raspy noise.

'I think because they were dressed just the way his boy used to be dressed. When Trouble was a puppy and he lived with his boy, the boy was almost always dressed like a sailor. He had bell bottomed trousers, white shirt and flat bottomed blue hat - most of the time. Very rarely clean, but that's what his mom liked to make him wear.

'And the boy, being a small boy and not caring much about clothes as long as they were comfortable, would wear his seaman uniform every day.'

'So Trouble had been looking for his boy all this time,' said the girl and was soon asleep.

Chapter 6

When old acquaintances meet

Next day came with rain and wind so all the outdoor activities had to be postponed much to Ana's delight for she wanted to hear more about Trouble and his story. But first, cookies had to be baked.

'Grandma,' said Ana after placing the breakfast dished in the sink, 'I want to do something nice for Grandad. I can see how much he enjoys telling us about his navy dog, Trouble, but it makes him sad at the same time. I don't understand.'

Grandma dried her hands on her apron and slowly sat at the table. She took hold of Ana's hand, pulling her closer. Ana enjoyed being near Grandma, it was comforting and safe and the girl liked the way Grandma smelled, sweet, like cookies and flour. And Grandma's hands, although wrinkled, were strong, yet soft at the same time. Softer than Mother's.

'Old and warm,' Tommy once said, snuggling with Grandma.

Grandma picked an invisible crumb from Ana's sleeve and absentmindedly straightened the girl's skirt.

'Sometimes, good memories can be both comforting and terrible at the same time. Do you remember your friend Simone, who moved to France last summer? When she writes to you, you are happy and sad at the same time. Why so you think?'

'I think I feel happy because her letters make me feel close to her again. Sad, because I couldn't hug her or spend time with her anymore, because she is so far away.'

'It is the same with Grandad's memories of youth. Remembering those happy times help him re-live them again, so he feels joyful. But not being able to be with his mates or with Trouble, not having their support and camaraderie, their encouragement anymore, that is sad. '

'I don't like it when Grandad is sad, but I really want to hear the rest of Trouble's story.'

'Don't worry, child. Grandad's memories may be cheerful and sad at the same time but the important part is that he looks back on those troublesome times with joy. And I think I know just how you can cheer him up.'

'How?'

Just then Tommy stormed into the kitchen.

'Cookies, can we bake cookies, Grandma? Please and thank you.'

Grandma waved towards the boy and smiled, 'Indeed we can.'

Grandma used a simple, basic recipe, yet her cookies never lasted too long.

That's why she would bake double the amount and hide half. There was nothing that made her happier than the smiles on her little one's faces, or Grandpa's, when they discovered that there was a secret stash of cookies just when they thought they ate the very last one.

First batch baked and Grandma chased them both away from her kitchen. The living room now seemed cool and inviting. Outside, it still rained. From the clouds, from the sky and even from the leafs. 'Will it ever stop,' thought Ana.

Tommy was there too, running around the room, chasing a ball.

'Grandad,' said Ana once they were both settled on the sofa, a plate of fresh cookies between them. 'How did you meet Trouble?'

'I met him on the train,' said the old man.

'Choo-choo train! I'm the engine,' exclaimed Tommy and he was soon a train himself, running along the living room, following the carpet's woven lines like some imaginary train tracks.

'Was it a train with lots of smoke, Grandad?'

'That's a steam train, Ana. Steam trains make loooooots of white smoke,' intervened Tommy and he stopped by the sofa, pulling an imaginary siren, 'Woo-woo!' and announced 'all aboard,' took a cookie and sped away.

Grandad waved after the train.

'No, it was an electric train. And

83

Trouble would often ride with us, seamen. For friendship, companionship and often,' coughed the old man, 'for titbits.'

'Titbits, Grandad? Like the ones Grandma gives us in the kitchen?' and the little girl licked her mouth.

'Titbits, like the ones Grandma gives you,' smiled the old man.

'Yum-yum!' exclaimed Tommy the train adding, 'I need supplies for my restaurant wagon,' so he changed direction leaving the room and heading for the kitchen.

'But why were you on the train, Grandad? Don't seamen belong... at sea?' said Ana.

'Of course they do, but when there isn't much work to be done or when seamen are very good, they get shore leave, or run-ashore, how we called it. So we would take the train to Cape Town and, quite often, Trouble would ride with us.

'It was a beautiful trip over green hills and in just under two hours we were in the biggest city any of us ever saw, Cape

Town. No wonder it was nick-named 'Mother City'. At that time it was considered the biggest city in the country, big enough to be a metropolis, they said. The name 'Mother City comes from the Greek 'metros', meaning mother and 'polis', meaning city. But there are other names Cape Town goes by and they, too, increased its magic for us. 'The Tavern of Seas', because European navigators stopped here on their sea travels to India following the Spice Route, particularly in search of black pepper. Or 'The Cape of Storms' or 'Cape of Good Hope' due to the rough waters and tumultuous winds that caused many vessels to become shipwrecked in its waters. Or 'Place of Sweet Water', how it is called by native

San people due to the many streams that run down Table Mountain nearby. Or 'Hui! Gaeb' meaning 'The Place Where The Clouds Gather' in Khoisan language, Khoi being another native tribe of this area. Because when clouds sit atop the nearby mountain, the Table Mountain, they look like a table cloth!

'But I guess Trouble accompanied us on our train journeys just for our company.'

'Where would he sit, Grandad?' said Ana, laughing.

'Well, he would sit on a bench, next to us. He was tall enough to sit his, ahem, behind on the train bench like any man would, while supporting himself upright with his front legs, his spine against the seat's backrest. And he would often like to look out of the window, to see the trees and the small towns go by.

'The carriages were stern and austere and quite cramped and were divided in compartments. If two people were seated face to face their knees were bound to touch. But the bench, seating four in each compartment, was soft and covered in dark green leather,' laughed Grandad. 'Luckily for us and Trouble as some carriages back then had hard, wooden benches. Now, it could get quite hot inside, especially when travelling during the long, sunny African summers, but although the carriages had only two doors, one at each end, and the compartments had sliding doors, the wagons displayed plenty of windows that stayed open throughout the train ride. So we had a cool breeze going.'

'He sat just like a human,' said Ana and she looked at grandad, sitting next to her on the sofa, his feet touching the carpet. Then she looked at her own feet, still hanging in the air.

'He was a tall dog, Grandad,' she said.

The old man stood up slowly and he stretched his back. He was still a tall man, towering over the little girl seated on the cushioned sofa.

'He was a tall dog indeed. When he was standing on his hind legs he could easily place his front paws on my shoulders and look me straight in the face, as easy as that.'

Then he sat back on the sofa and slapped his knee in excitement.

'Yes, Trouble was a fine dog. But,' he added in a serious voice, 'even dogs need a ticket when they ride in the train - especially big dogs.'

The girl's eyebrows rose towards the ceiling.

'He didn't have a ticket?'

'Well, how could he? He didn't have money. He just wanted to be with us, his friends. We were his pack, his family. He felt like he belonged with us. And he would often keep us safe.'

'Like he kept his boy safe,' whispered Ana. 'Maybe he didn't know he needed a ticket?'

'Of course he didn't. But dogs weren't allowed to ride in trains, it was against the rules and so Trouble was often put off. Yet, he never made a fuss, nor did he fight the Ticket Collectors. Sometimes we, sailors, would try to hide him from the train authorities, but that was practically impossible since he was such a large dog.'

'Where would you hide him, Grandad?'

A wide smile covered the man's face.

'Sometimes we would get him to lie on the bench and we would sit in front of him, on the edge, hiding him behind. Other times we would try to hide him underneath the bench. But he was so big, a paw or his tail, usually waging, would

91

always stick out. And the Ticket Collector would almost always find him and threaten that such a dog did not belong in his trains, nor in the navy, but in the Davy Jones' Locker - and that meant at the bottom of the sea.'

'Oh, no! Poor, poor dog. I surely hope he couldn't understand everything the Ticket Collector said about him. And then?'

'It depends on who was on duty that day. You can say Trouble had a sense for the person. Sometimes Trouble would stand on his hind legs and place his large, heavy front paws on the conductor's shoulders. Then he would growl into the poor man's face and the Ticket Collector's face would change from red to white, not knowing what to expect next. For not many people understand what a dog means when he growls.'

'Do you, Grandad?'

'Well, maybe I can't read any dog, but I knew Trouble and I could tell what he meant when he would growl. For example with the Collector, his growl was low and soft, yet the hair on the back of his head was smooth, not raised and his tail was kept low and relaxed, wagging just a little. His eyes were focused on the man's face. To me, that growl meant 'I am a good dog, I don't understand what you have against me, but I will try to cooperate.'

Ana nearly fell off the sofa with laughter. 'All that, Grandad? Was Trouble saying all that with just one growl?'

93

'Of course. Dogs can speak in whole sentences if you only pay attention. And Trouble did just that. This would amuse the civilians riding in the train so much, that they would even offer to pay for the dog's train ticket! Of course, the Ticket Collector would never accept it and he would just chase Trouble out of train at the first stop.'

'Wasn't he getting lost, then?' said Ana.

'Remember how he helped his boy return home? Trouble had a fine nose for a dog. And for dogs, smelling is the way they map the world. They can tell between the different odours that surround us, but also find a scent that is present only in the air and track it, follow it. I think humans were able to smell a lot better a very, very long time ago. But as we evolved and began to speak, we lost some of our sniffing abilities to make space for new skills such as singing, hunting, thinking, planning. Perhaps that's why humans began taming wolves in the first place. Because wolves could do one thing so much more better than us, smelling. Remember, dogs descend from wolves. For dogs, using their smell abilities is like us looking for answers in a book. When meeting a new person, we introduce ourselves. Dogs, they sniff each other and know exactly if they meet a girl or a boy, a puppy or an old dog, even if the dog they meet is healthy or sick. And they react accordingly.'

A flicker of amusement lit up in the old man's eyes.

'Yes, Trouble has a fine nose for a dog. Also, not to worry. Sometimes, just as the Ticket Collector would turn his back, Trouble would quickly re-enter the carriage. He would simply jump inside through an open window.'

'Jump through a train window?' Ana

couldn't believe it. 'But that's high!'

'Not too high for Trouble. He was determined not to be parted with his friends. And if he couldn't jump back in the train, he would simply catch the next one.'

Ana thought of the last time she'd been in a train station. She was holding tight onto Grandma's hand while Grandad was holding Tommy. She liked trains, but she didn't like how busy train stations were. Full of people going in all directions, big luggage standing everywhere, smoke and dust. And noise, lots of noise.

'Wasn't the noise bothering Trouble? Train stations are so noisy.'

'You know what, maybe it did. I never

thought of that for I never saw Trouble to flinch because of a noise. But dogs do hear on a wider range than humans do. They hear sounds so high that we can't even hear them and they can hear very, very low sounds too, sounds that humans aren't able to hear either.

'So, how did Trouble found his way around? You know, at that time there were 27 stations between Simon's Town, where the Naval Base was located and where Trouble and us lived and Cape Town, where us, seamen, liked to spend our free time when on shore leave. Such a big distance, yet Trouble always knew where to go and which way was home. And if thrown out of a train at any of these stations he would always catch the right train again. Probably because he liked his friends with blue bell-bottomed trousers, square blue collars and flat topped naval caps so much.'

'I think he had a good nose,' exclaimed the little girl. 'He could sniff the fish in the Ocean from miles away. Still, how did he know which direction to go, Grandad?'

The old man laughed and thought for a moment.

'I guess it was in his nature. He was a very clever dog, determined not to be parted with his friends. You must remember this.'

Grandad was now serious as he looked straight into Ana's eyes.

'Determination and faith, Ana, will

always get you through tough times. Always.'

'Did the seamen loved Trouble too?'

'Oh, yes, very much so.'

'Was it hard to be a seamen during war, Grandad?'

'It is difficult to be away from home at any time, but most so during war time. One never knows… one never knows what each day brings. But one thing's for sure, Trouble brought us all joy, day in and day out.

'War time is a different time. You feel like you don't have the same control over your life. There are different rules, you get to do something else altogether, away from your family and your life the way you knew it before war started.

100

'This dog brought us something positive to focus on. And when we would forget the personal reasons for which we enrolled in the navy, because when you get muddled about something you tend to forget why you chose to be there in the first place, then, Trouble would remind us of why we were there. To keep our loved ones safe, to serve our country, to fight the bad folk.

'Trouble, with his heart of gold, reminded us of our own hearts, of our own hopes and dreams for the future. And that is something worth fighting for.'

'I wonder if other soldiers also had dogs that brought them smiles,' said Ana.

'Bless your heart, girl! Indeed they did. During the war, but mostly after,

101

people would hear amazing stories about brave, wonderful dogs, horses and donkeys too, that helped the soldiers on the battlefield and behind it.

'Some dogs were messengers and couriers. They helped deliver secret messages, especially smaller, brown dogs easy to camouflage themselves. Some dogs even carried on their backs cages with homing pigeons, pigeons that were then sent back home, behind the lines, with secret, important messages attached to their feet.

'Some dogs were working for the Red Cross. They were lifesaving ambulance dogs and had to perform some of the most dangerous missions. They would carry medical packs in a special saddle fixed on their back. On the saddle there was a red cross, so everyone would know this is a medical dog. Their job was to find the wounded soldiers and give them the medical supplies so that they can help themselves. If the soldier was too injured, the dog would bring his cap back to the medic, the medic would write down the wounded soldier's name from inside the cap and then he would follow the dog to the injured warrior.

'Other such dogs were trained as watchdogs, doing the job of a sentry, a scout or a guard. Because of their keen senses, hearing, smelling and sight, these dogs would raise the alarm during the night if enemy was approaching. But they would not bark, rather growl softly or just stand. If they were patrolling, the dogs could smell the enemy and, quietly, alert his soldier.

'But the funniest ones were the mascot dogs. These were dogs found by soldiers in abandoned houses, dogs that suddenly began following a group of warriors or, sometimes, a dog that belonged to someone higher in rank but had been adopted by the entire regiment. Some mascots were not even dogs, they were goats, ponies, monkeys. What they all managed to do, unbeknownst to them, was bridging the gap between war and home, keep the soldiers connected with one another, keep the care and the laughter going. There are times at war when words don't help. A dog can help with only a wag of his tail or a lick of the hand. Dogs were lfe savers during war time.'

Funny noises were coming from the kitchen. Pots and pans and Grandma's voice and Tommy's short exclamations, every now and then.

Ana smiled.

'He seems determined,' she said and they both laughed.

Just then Tommy burst through the door, holding a cooking pan and a wooden spoon. He looked happy. His mouth was shiny and there was something red on his chin.

'Jam,' thought Ana.

Grandma was making vetkoek (those delicious, tasty, huge doughnuts) for lunch.

Tommy ran across the living room holding the pot and the spoon he forcefully removed from the kitchen. The tail of his toy dog was tucked into his pants. He would never be parted from him.

Ana thought of Trouble's own boy who had to go to school and leave his own dog behind. 'Did he had a choice,' she wondered.

Tommy's dog could fit in any suitcase, even Mother's purse in case of an emergency.

The toy dog was bouncing with every step Tommy was laughing, proclaiming 'lunch, lunch, lunch for all, you better be hungry.'

Just then the toy dog fell to the floor. Tommy tried not to step on it, while still balancing the pot and the spoon. The pot fell with a bang and slid to Grandad's feet. The spoon rolled under a chair.

Tommy was up again, tucking half of his toy dog into his pants the same time Grandad picked up the container. Three heads peered inside the pot.

'Lunch,' explained Tommy with a satisfied look on his face, 'for you and you and you…and me' and he pointed towards Ana, Grandad, his own toy dog and then himself.

Inside the cooking pot there were three vetkoekke spread with jam.

'Tommy, how did you convinced Grandma to part with these vetkoekke so soon before lunch?' asked Grandad.

'You have to have a backstory to why you need to eat right before lunch, right?' said Tommy. 'I love vetkoekke. They are filled with jam and dreams.'

'Determination,' smiled Grandad. 'Thank you, Tommy.'

Chapter 7

A sea of letters

'So that's how you got to know Joyful Trouble,' said Ana.

The last bite of her vetkoek was now gone. She has also enjoyed a piece of Grandad's and was licking her fingers.

'How and where I met him. In a train, sharing my lunch. You know, when I first met Trouble he ate half of my food,' said Grandad.

'Hungry!' exclaimed Tommy, patting his stomach.

'Yes, he was hungry. But he was also

big,' said Grandad. 'That day Trouble ate half of my lunch and half of the lunch of every seaman in my group. And we were eight!'

'Were your friends upset, then?' said Ana.

'No. They laughed and shared. Trouble was such a gentle dog and his brown eyes were so soft and tender when he was looking at you, then at your food, then at you again. And then,' said Grandad with a smile, 'if you still ignored him, he would sigh and lean his big, warm heavy head on your knee and sigh some more. And he would look up at you, then sideways, then up at you again and you would hear 'drip, drip' and at first you wouldn't know what it is, but you would hear it again, faster, 'drip, drip, drip,' and then you would realise that it is the dog's saliva dripping on the compartment floor. He was drooling because of your food and you would end up feeling sorry for him....'

'And give him half of your lunch,' said Ana and she laughed, clapping her hands.

'Indeed you would.'

'And when there weren't many of us, seamen, in the train wagon to feed him, Trouble would get food from the civilians riding in the train. Nobody minded feeding him a bit. And a bit from many people made just a meal that was enough for Trouble.'

'Titbits,' said Ana.

'Titbits! Bringing some right now,' exclaimed Tommy and ran out of the room again.

Grandad gently laid the empty pot on the table.

'These free train rides Trouble was taking soon made the South African Railway Officials so mad that they went about snooping, found out who his real owner was and warned him, with more than just one written letter, that if he did not control his dog and take him off the trains, they will have to put the dog down!'

One look towards the girl's concerned face and the story moved on at a quicker pace.

'Of course, nothing bad happened to

Trouble because something amazing happened instead. Actually two amazing things happened almost at once.

'People from far away, from all over the Cape Peninsula, sailors too, they all wrote to the authorities, especially to the Commander-in-Chief of the Navy. For friends in need are friends indeed and now it was the people's turn to show they were good friends of our dog.'

Grandad slapped his knees in excitement.

'During a single week after the Railway Officials' warning came out there were so many letters written, that extra postmen had to be appointed to deliver them. And the Commander-in-Chief of the Navy had a pile so big on his desk, that if you would enter his room you wouldn't be able to see the man sitting behind, on his chair.'

Ana glanced towards her mother's writing desk by the window.

'Some letters were short, as short as two words, "Save Trouble!" - so they seemed to be a coded message if you didn't know better. Some were formal, with a letter-header and typed on a typewriter. Some were elaborate letters, written on beautiful paper in crafty hand writing while some were written on a corner torn from a newspaper.' And Grandad held out his palms together, as if holding something precious.

'Some letters were written by simple people, like us, seamen. The writing was clumsy and the letters were formed with difficulty. Some were written by children, in big, sloppy words. Some were elegant and even smelled of perfume. Some were signed with the full name and an address, some just with the first name and some with only an initial. And there were even letters written on top of another letter;

people often did that during war times, to save paper.'

Ana's eyebrows went high. She wanted to ask how this was possible, how people could not have enough paper to write on, but she didn't want the story to stop.

'You see, the Cook had seen the pile of letters on the captain's desk when he went to check the week's menu. And he came running to the canteen with the good news. And the Surgeon had seen them too and he told the Surgeon's mate, who told the carpenter, who told the sailmaker, who told his mate, who told us all, able and ordinary seamen. And soon everybody in the naval base and dockyards knew about them. And even more letters were written.

'You could feel the excitement in the air. People were smiling more than usual; they would pat each other's back and laugh. We had a common goal, a purpose other than the navy life during war; and it was making us all happy. Here,' and he pointed towards his heart.

'You know what was amazing about those letters?'

'That there were so many?'

'Yes, yes, but also that everyone was

asking for the same thing. Civilians and seamen, young or old, women and men, they were all asking the Commander-in-Chief to save this amazing dog, their friend. My friend too.'

'You also wrote a letter, Grandad?' said Ana and her face lit up.

'I also wrote a letter. My shipmates and I wrote a special petition to the Commander. You see, we didn't know that the civilians would also write to help Trouble. We were feeling a bit guilty for causing this great dog such misfortune. It was because of us, after all, that he'd been riding the trains in the first place.'

Grandad smiled.

'And with all the letters sent to the authorities and to the Commander-in-

Chief of the South Atlantic Navy, this is how it came that the Commander decided to take matters into his own hands and make justice.'

'And what did he do?' said Ana.

'The rain stopped, the rain stopped, the rain stopped...' said Tommy, rushing in and running all around the living room, only to disappear in the hallway again.

'I'm going to have a meeting with my puddles, Grandad, come.'

Grandad smiled, 'aye,aye.'

'I guess we better go out for a walk. And I'll tell you the story further.'

Chapter 8

The Enrolling Ceremony

The air outside was cool and moist and it smelled of earth and leaves, clean and sweet.

Tommy made it for the first puddle. He looked at it, concentration painted all over his face, then he bend.

'I found a starfish in the puddle,' he soon declared. 'No, wait, it was my hand.'

He stood still for a moment, holding his ball above his head. Then, shouting 'aim, splash,' he threw the ball right in the middle of the pool. He didn't jump away, he didn't even flinch. He just closed his eyes.

Muddy droplets covered the entire front of his blue rain boots, of his knee-length yellow rain coat and... his face.

The boy smiled.

'Good splash, ten out of nine,' he said and wiped his face with the wet sleeve of his coat. The muddy droplets turned into muddy streaks. And so, war-like painted, Tommy made it for the nearest bush.

'Long stick, long stick, where are you?' he said and the ball was left behind, queen of her own puddle; but not for long.

Ana and Grandad watched Tommy from the top of the front steps. If Mom or Grandma were not around to worry and fuss over clean clothes, Ana knew that Grandad would just make sure that Tommy was safe, as well as having a great time.

'Clothes and little boys are made to be washed,' he would always say.

Not that everyone was happy with his reasoning, as Grandma would always emphasize.

'Now, remember when I said that two amazing things happened? Besides the humans writing all those letters Trouble did something too.'

'What did he do, Grandad? Oh, no,' exclaimed the girl, a worried look over her face.

'Now, child,' laughed Grandad, 'have a little faith in our dog. So it happened that one day, while Trouble was walking about the town, he passed a house with white washed walls, thatched roof, a front door with an beautiful window pane above and wooden shutters on each one of the two lateral windows, one on each side of the door. If you ask me, the house seemed to have a face of her own. But

123

that's not what made Trouble stop. It was his keen hearing. He stopped as if he hit a brick wall and he began to bark and bark. It was completely out of character for him to bark like that and I realized it right away.

'For so it happened that I was on my way back to the ship when I heard the commotion. I tried to pull him away, I even tried to hold his mouth closed using both my hands, but to no avail. I even tried to bribe him with the little bit of biltong I carried in my pockets. And I knew how fond of biltong Trouble was! Nothing could lure him away. He would bark at that house and even add an additional whining, something I've never heard him produce before. And he would pull at the bottom of my pants and try to drag me towards the house.

'Finally I gave in, summoned my courage and approached the front door. The house looked spick and span and I was only a seamen. I could only imagine who lived there, the height of the society for sure. How was I to explain that a mad, giant dog named Trouble told me to knock at their door? I felt so silly, yet I trusted my four legged friend.

'But as soon as I approached the door I could hear muffled cries for help. I knocked and called, yet no one came to open. Back then people were not locking their doors so I let myself inside. As soon as I opened the door Trouble bolted for the back of the house where the old woman that lived there lay on a heap on the floor. She had fallen of a ladder and broken her leg. Needless to say, Trouble was the hero of the day. But that was not all. The old woman was no one else but the Ticket Collector's mother. He was so happy and so ashamed when he found out the story!'

'Why was he ashamed, Grandad?'

'I think because he treated Trouble so badly and in return the dog saved his mother. The dog proved to be the better person.'

'Of course, this wonderful piece of news got to the Commander-in-Chief pretty soon. And the Commander-in-Chief, given all that had happened lately, decided that the best way forward was to officially enlist Trouble into the Royal Navy, as Ordinary Seaman.

'It was Friday, the 25th of August 1939, when this Great Dane and wonderful friend was officially inducted into the Royal Navy at the recruiting office of the HMS Afrikander III. And this was the precise day the Commander-in-Chief had called me into his office. The day I walked in to find Trouble comfortably sitting at the Commander's desk.'

'Have you seen this dog before?' the Commander asked me and Trouble pressed his lips together rolling his eyes sideways, away from the Commanders' eyes and my own, keeping his ears alert.

'What did that mean, Grandad?' laughed Ana and tears rolled down her cheeks.

'In dog language it meant 'it is all your doing, I always mind my own business. Suit yourself.'

'So I said aye, aye, Commander, Sir, I have seen this dog before,' without giving away too much detail.

'You are well aware of the situation this dog has caused around the town, Seaman?' had asked the Commander further. So I said yes, I was.

'I have decided to enrol this dog into the Royal Navy,' said the Commander, 'but I am enlisting you, Able Seaman, with the task of washing Trouble regularly, of making sure that his cap and collar won't go missing, and also with making sure you keep Ordinary Seaman

Trouble, here, under control.'

'At this Trouble, still sitting on the chair, dropped his chin into his chest and snorted. In agreement, I thought.

'Soon after that the Midshipman walked in with the registration log and the enlisting process began.

'The Commander looked at Trouble, then looked at the carpet by my feet and, if I wasn't witnessing I wouldn't have believed it in a million years. Trouble jumped down from the Commander's chair and came to sit right by my feet. He sat bold upright on his bottom, tail neatly tucked in and I could swear he even tucked his tummy in, his nose pointed up in salute.

'The Commander took his place at his

desk and the registration process began, the desk being used again for its intended purpose.

'Surname? said the Midshipman.

'Trouble,' said the Commander, 'because he always seems to get himself in trouble.' And he looked sternly towards the dog.'

'And the dog?' giggled Ana.

'He kept his cool. He knew, you see, that it was an important moment. So he behaved.'

'Such a clever dog,' smiled the girl cupping her cheeks and shaking her head the way Mother did when Tommy had done it.

'Indeed he was clever. He only barked once in agreement.

'The Midshipman wrote down the name.

'Christian name? said the Midshipman further.

'At this the Commander looked at me for an answer. You see, the enrolment form was made for humans and all humans have a surname and a Christian name. At that moment I remembered all the laughter and joy Trouble had brought us all.

'Joyful, Sir,' I said and Trouble barked again.

'The Midshipman looked up in surprise, but the Commander smiled and nodded in agreement. 'A well suited name indeed,' and the Midshipman wrote down the Christian name.

131

'Trade? said the Midshipman further.

'Because on a ship everyone has his own job, his own trade. It helps you know what is expected of you and where you belong. And it keeps things tidy and in order. Navy people like this very much.

'Bone crusher,' smiled the Commander after taking one look at Trouble.

'And did Trouble bark again, Grandad?'

'Twice. I think he wholeheartedly agreed.'

'And the Midshipman wrote it down?'

'With a smile.'

'Religion? said the Midshipman next.

The Commander sighed and looked at Trouble.

'You're a very resourceful canine, Trouble,' said the Commander. 'You got the whole town and the entire crew of this Naval Base on your side on such a short time. Even the newspapers, the mail services and the Railway Officials. Put down Scrounger,' he said towards the Midshipman.'

'And Trouble, did he bark again?'

'Indeed he did. And he didn't mind one bit to be called a scrounger. Because sometimes, under the right circumstances, even bad names have a silver lining to them,' said Grandad.

'Muddy me, muddy me,' sang Tommy, now running right through the puddle, kicking the ball and waving a stick. Then his feet slid through the mud and the boy

133

regained his balance at the last moment.

'I just scared myself half-alive. Boy, I am so tired, and so broke.'

Ana and Grandad looked at each other and smiled, a meaningful smile.

'Then the Midshipman scratched his head, looking in the direction of the dog.'

'Commander,' he said, 'the dog needs to sign the application form or it won't be legal.'

'And what did the Commander do?' said Ana, trying hard not to laugh.

'Well, the Commander, in his smart uniform and perfectly pressed pants, picked up the registration form and the ink bottle from the desk, kneeled on the carpet, then took and dipped Trouble's right paw into the ink so that he can press it on the document and sign. His very own Ordinary Seaman Certificate.'

'Now, take Ordinary Seamen Joyful Trouble to have his medical done, Seaman,' he said to me and we were out and into the corridor in no time.'

'He had to have his medical?'

'His medical examination, yes. No one can be enrolled into the navy without passing his medical.'

'And did he?'

'Of course he did; Trouble was as fit as a fiddle. With all the walking between stations and jumping in and out of train wagons, he was a very fit dog.

'But it's been rather difficult to make our way to the medical room because the corridors and the yard were full with seamen and other Navy personnel. They all heard something was happening and they all wanted to see what, what was the Commander's decision regarding Trouble?'

'And were they happy?'

'Happy? They were over the moon! It is a tough life being in the army during war, any army, be it navy, air corps, artillery, away from family and home, worrying about their well-being without being able to do much about it but write to them, often feeling lonely, having to share a small space with lots of other men just as worried as you... When something extraordinary happens it tends to feel like Christmas.

'So, as soon as the Commander came out of his office they picked him up and carried him around just like a hero. And they cheered and clapped for him.

'This was not very military, but the men were so happy and grateful! Then, as soon as they put him down again, they

137

all stood silent in salute, hundreds of them, because their beloved Trouble was finally safe. And as a Navy Seaman he now also had a free pass on the train!

'So after he'd been declared fit for duty Trouble and I went to fetch his new seaman's cap and new collar, which had been etched with his name, rank and number. It was a fine leather collar with metal studs and a plate that read 'Joyful Trouble, O.R-1, H.M.S. Afrikander I, Simon's Town.'

'So many letters, what do they all meant?'

'O.R-1 was his navy rank, it means Ordinary Seaman rank 1, the lowest rank in the navy, a junior rank and some call it a matelot or a matrose. Only a seamen with less than two years' experience at sea and who shows enough seamanship can be an ordinary seaman and rated so by the captain. A seaman with less than a year's experience is called a landsman, so you see what a great honour the Commander-in-Chief bestowed upon Joyful Trouble. Now ordinary seaman are not trained in any particular task, but required to do any physical task, of any variety, which was exactly what Joyful Trouble was doing, him being everywhere, all the time.

'And H.M.S. Afrikander was the name of our ship, a fine coastal gunboat and one of the first ships without masts, because we had a gun on board. It was part of the Royal Navy flotilla, H.M.S.

meaning 'Her Majesty's Ship.'

Ana thought of her little brother and of the way he always lost his cap.

'How did you make Joyful Trouble's hat to sit on his head, Grandad?'

'He lost it many times and a seaman must wear his complete uniform when performing a task, any task, at any time. And if you don't, no matter the cause, you brake a navy law plus you have to pay for the lost piece of uniform from your own wedges and do extra hours of duty.

'And Joyful Trouble paid?'

'Well, let's just say he got a lot less bones to chew on whenever he lost his seaman cap.'

'Did he like it?'

'Not one bit. So one day I just sewed a strap that would go underneath his chin to keep his seaman cap tightly in place.'

Ana squinted.

141

'And he liked it?'

'Not at first, but a few titbits convinced him to keep it on,' said Grandad with a smile.

'Watch,' he said and he approached Tommy.

Ana observed from a safe distance. She knew from experience that her little brother was a danger to her clean clothes whenever he was found near a puddle, or a ball, or a stick. And now he owned all three.

Ana watched Grandad approaching the boy, then bending over and talking to Tommy, listening in return and then talking some more. Then she saw Grandad pointing towards the house, then towards his wrist watch, then towards the puddle. She wondered what would happen next. Mother always ended up chasing Tommy around the yard before catching him; Grandma always called Mother who seemed to enjoy a game of catch with the little boy, while Dad simply picked him up to avoid any argument.

To her amazement, she saw Tommy pick up his ball and walk towards the house all by himself. But not towards the front door that opened on the clean carpet; but instead heading towards the side door, that opened in the small, tiled hallway neighbouring the kitchen and the extra bathroom.

'How did you do it?' exclaimed the girl.

Grandad smiled as he walked past her.

He said only one word.

'Titbits.'

Chapter 9

Old friends reunited

It was bedtime again.

Ana was under the duvet, her head resting on the pillow, but she was watching Grandad, seated next to the bed, with eager eyes. And Tommy was in bed too, on top of the duvet. With his toy dog placed on his head he was lying on his tummy, one leg bend at the knee, the other one hanging out of bed. He, too, was facing Grandad, yet his eyes were wandering around the room when he suddenly proclaimed:

'I have stinky winds, but they are silent. Not so bad. Apologies for any harm caused. And thank you.'

'Story, Grandad?' asked Ana wrinkling her nose.

'Story, you say,' said Grandad patting his chin and eyeing the ceiling thoughtfully.

'Doggie story, doggie story,' exclaimed Tommy, still balancing his toy dog on top of his head.

'Doggie story?' asked Grandad surprised. 'Now, I wonder which one shall it be tonight.'

Ana burst into laughter.

'Joyful Trouble, Grandad,' she said.

'You like the navy dog, child?' The old man patted her head.

'Ordinary Seadog,' said Ana.

'Ordinary Sea-dog,' said Grandad slowly then he laughed too. 'Yes, I believe you can call him that, after all he had the rank of Ordinary Seaman!'

147

'Woof, woof,' said a voice by Grandad's feet.

The old man glanced towards the floor and smiled. Ana leaned over to take a look.

'What have we here?' said Grandad with pretend surprise, 'but an Ordinary Seadog!'

Tommy had been crawling all around the bed, his seaman cap on his head.

'Woof, woof,' he said again, pretending to pant just like a dog. One of his legs went up and it moved back and forth, doing an imaginary dog-scratch motion.

'Well, little doggie, would you like a bone?' said Grandad and the dog shook his head.

'Would you like a little scratch behind your ear?' said Grandad again.

The doggie considered it for a moment then shook his head again, panting.

'Would you like a story?'

'Woof, woof, story!' barked the pup.

Ana giggled from bed.

'I'm afraid we have a talking puppy, Grandad.'

'Lucky us,' said the old man, smiling knowingly, 'lucky us indeed.' And he helped the pyjama wearing dog climb into his lap.

Ana stretched and kissed his head. 'You small like a puppy, Tommy.'

'Thank you.'

'Joyful Trouble was a dog just like

149

you, a talking dog,' began Grandad.

'Could he really talk, Grandad?' said Tommy with big eyes.

'Not in human words, but in dog words. His face and body could tell you a lot, and he always made himself understood. Like this one time...' Grandad began.

Ana clapped and Tommy-dog clapped too.

'You see, Joyful Trouble took his naval service very seriously. If a fight ever broke out, and arguments often sparked when mariners were cooped up on land for too long, Joyful Trouble was there to stop it right away. It was in his blood, you can say. He didn't like to see people fighting. He was at his happiest when everyone was getting along.'

'I don't like fights,' whispered Tommy.

'Me neither. Grandad, how did Joyful Trouble knew when people were fighting?'

'I think he could sense the people were upset, unhappy, frustrated. His ears would drop, his tongue would stick out and look so wide you would think it can never fit back in his mouth. His eyes would be narrow, like he would measure you. His ears would go up and back and then the hairs on the back of the neck would rise and he would begin to growl, like he's had it with you, you must stop this nonsense.

'And what would he do then, Grandad?' said Ana.

151

'He would usually go and snuggle with the least strong opponent, nuzzle him, curl up and sleep.'

'Sleep,' echoed Tommy and closed his eyes.

It was warm in Grandad's arms.

The story went on in a softer voice.

'That's why when a fight broke out Joyful Trouble was sure to stop it right way.

'He wouldn't bite, no. Some other times he would walk towards the two opponents and he would stop and stand right between them. Then he would growl, with low, long rumbles and quite loud, without looking at either of them because he would growl at both of them. He would ask them both, loud and clear,

152

to stop the fight, stop the nonsense, we are all friends here. It wasn't an aggressive growling, but a polite warning. And then, he would choose one of them, usually the tallest one, or the strongest one, and he would place his front paws on his shoulders.'

Ana's eyebrows rose. She looked at

Tommy, sleeping in Grandad's lap; she looked at his toy dog, asleep too in his own lap.

'Remember the dog you made friends with at the parade? The one who was standing in front of you and whose eyes were level with yours? And whose nose was level with your own?'

Ana rubbed her nose absentminded.

'His breath smelled funny. It smelled of grass and of something else…'

Grandad smiled.

'Joyful Trouble was a dog just like that one, a Great Dane. Now imagine that parade dog standing. He could easily put his front paws on my chest and look me in the eye because he is so tall.'

'But you're so big, Grandad! You're

the tallest Grandad I know!'

The old man smiled. He wasn't young anymore, but it made him feel young, in a silly way, hearing that he's the tallest Grandad. Or at least that his little granddaughter thought he was. That was enough for him.

'You know that we measured Joyful Trouble once, while he was standing? We wanted to see how tall he was. Silly seamen we were! But he was a good dog, he didn't mind.'

'Really? And how tall was he?'

'He was almost, almost 2 meters tall.'

'That's tall, Grandad!' exclaimed Ana then quickly repeated in a softer tone, 'that's tall.'

'Indeed it is. Now imagine this great

dog's face suddenly level with your own, but you're a grown-up and you're standing and looking into this big, hairy face pasted right in front of yours. And imagine feeling the weight of this dog's body on your shoulders. Wouldn't you stop any argument?

'Joyful Trouble wouldn't bark, no. He would only watch the man in the eye with his own soft, gentle brown eyes, calm from underneath a pair of bushy eyebrows. Not mad in the least, just curious and loving. And then the man would get a whiff of Trouble's breath smelling of whatever the dog had eaten last - and most of the time that was fish.

'The compact weight and heat of his big canine body together with his intense stare and mouth odour were enough to make any seaman, no matter how angry, instantly cool down.

'Well, THAT was a sight to remember!

'And this is how Joyful Trouble got any fight to stop.'

Ana studied her Grandad thoughtfully.

'How do you know this so well, Grandad? Were YOU ever in a fight?'

The old man coughed.

'Now, maybe not as much a fight as an argument of some sorts,' he said then went on.

'Joyful Trouble helped his mates in countless other ways.

'Sometimes, late at night, when seamen were leaving the pub and were too tired to walk back to base, Trouble

157

would accompany them, even allowing them to hold onto his strong back for support.

'But many times he was riding the train with us. The Ticket Collectors could say nothing against him for now he was one of us, complete with a seaman's hat and number, plus he had begun to like Trouble and appreciate him, especially his sniffing abilities.'

Grandad glanced towards the clock.

'The men loved him and everyone on the docks or at the base was a lot happier now that Joyful Trouble was one of us. He was our mascot, you could say, our good luck charm and even more because we were at war. He was one of us, a trusting mate. His mere presence provided us all with a homing sense of calm.

'Watching him enjoying himself in the moment, lazily taking a sun bath, reminded us to take joy in the simple things found in the present, duel less about the families left behind or the future worries of war. Even watching him go for a stroll was enlightening. Like any dog when he walked, he walked. You could see how much he enjoyed being alive, taking in the sights, the sounds and the smells. His legs would move in a cheerful rhythm, his tail would swish, his bum would hop along and this reminded us to cherish being alive ourselves and to count our blessings rather than dwell in our losses.

'Although we were not fighting yet, war had broken out in Europe and we, seamen, were in a navy base, away from families and loved ones. Having a dog with us was making us feel closer to home. Having Joyful Trouble there was like having a bit of our own homes with us, in the Navy base.

'With him there, amongst us, we all felt more like a family and less like soldiers. Joyful Trouble's presence was like an assurance that, one day, we will all have our own dogs, our own families, our own civilian lives back.

'And it was good to know that.'

Grandad was quiet for a moment as his eyes were looking over Tommy's head, towards a place far away. Ana knew he was not looking at the wall behind her bed. She wondered if Grandad missed Joyful Trouble.

'That's why,' Grandad picked up the story again, 'for his dedicated service

Joyful Trouble was soon promoted to the rank of Able Seaman or A.B, together with a brand new collar and cap. This meant he would get his own food ratio and he could even sit and eat together with his seamen, on the mess deck. One of the first things Joyful Trouble learned as an Able Seamen was the call of the Boatswain Pipe, the call that announced the meals aboard and the shortest way to galley, where the ship's kitchen is.

'Of course, now he would even get his own bed in one of the huts, together with the boys, and receive shore leave!

'In many ways Joyful Trouble was to us all, in the navy:

'A dog before a messmate,

A messmate before a shipmate,

162

A shipmate before a stranger.'

Ana giggled, 'he had his own pillow too, Grandad?'

'His own pillow too.

'My job, now, was to make sure Joyful Trouble was washed regularly, clean at all times and that he'd appear in parades and at official functions in the aid of the Navy - with his cap on! Through his mere presence at official parades he helped recruit quite a big number of sailors. The Royal Navy was especially looking to increase its numbers during those years. And he also helped with donations towards the navy, something that was always most welcomed.

'My bed was right next to his and I would often wake up in the middle of the night to see Joyful Trouble asleep in his own bed, all stretched out, and with his head on the pillow.

'He had never slept with a pillow before, at least not since he'd been with us. But look, now he was quite fond of it!'

'Maybe he remembered his boy's pillow, Grandad,' said Ana softly.

'Indeed, perhaps he did. He dreamed too, that's for sure. For how else can you explain his quivering, leg twitching, even soft growling during his sleep? I am sure he was dreaming about things that happened to him throughout the day.'

The little girl laughed and the old man laughed and the stars and the moon and all the stuffed toys aligned at the foot of the bed laughed as well.

Only Tommy snored softly, his own toy dog tucked under his chin.

'Time for bed, little sailor,' smiled Grandad and he removed the flat-topped naval cap from the boy's head.

Then, ever so careful and very slowly

he got up from his chair, while still cradling Tommy, and walked around the bed.

'Grandad, you and God are a lot alike,' whispered the little boy peering through his half closed eyelids.

'Oh, how is that?'

'You're both old and loving.'

Ana smiled at Grandad's smile stretched across his red cheeks and helped by undoing the bed covers and fluffing up her brother's pillow.

'Grandad, how did he get his name in the first place, Trouble?'

'Oh, that!' laughed the old man softly.

'That's a story for tomorrow.

Chapter 10

Give this dog a name and a bone

Next day Father came home from his weekly trip so the children were much too excited not to spend the entire day with him.

And at bedtime they were too exhausted to keep their eyes open. Even for a Joyful Trouble story.

'I need to go to bed,' complained Tommy. 'This week was so long.'

'Mom, why don't we have dogs?' said Ana.

'Dad is allergic to dog hair, sweetie.'

'He could sleep outside,' offered Tommy.

'The dog?'

'No, daddy,' explained the boy half asleep.

Then it was the weekend which brought along visitors, aunts and cousins, long, never-ending meals and lots of cakes for dessert. Much more than in a normal week day!

'Jams and jellies, jams and jellies,' Tommy was shouting at the top of his voice while running around the living room.

'Guess what I am going to put on my peanut butter and jam sandwich?'

'What?'

'Jam and peanut butter!'

Then Ana's cookies, just like Grandma's but with a twist, were baked again so Dad can take a whole tin with him in his weekly trip and not miss home that much.

It was Monday when things went back to normal, back into their own trail. Just like a river that's been overflowing its banks after a good rain and now runs in its banks again, re-energized by the rain, surprised by its own strength.

'You saw that, you saw me,' he seems to be saying, 'that's how far I went! Look, all the way to that tree over there! I watered it and now, look, there's grass growing there again. And as far as those bushes on the other side. See how far I got, how wide I could spread?'

It was a sunny Monday so Tommy, Ana and Grandad went to the stream running behind their house.

Tommy, in shorts and shirt, was running ahead jumping, his hands hungry for sticks and stones, his eyes searching the ground.

Ana was carrying a blanket, walking at Grandad's pace. His knee had been sore lately, so he was walking slower than usual. It was his injured knee, Ana remembered. She looked towards it with worry. Still, Grandad insisted on carrying the picnic basket. And a good idea that was for Grandma had been stuffing it.

'Enough to feed an army,' she had said and had laughed lovingly at

Grandad.

'But we're only three,' said Ana.

'That's an army,' said Grandma, 'my army,' and she smiled giving Ana a hug.

'Bang, bang!' echoed Tommy.

Ana chose a spot in the shade and

laid down the blanket then arranged the tablecloth on top of it and began sorting the food.

She first offered Grandad some biscuits.

'Haven't we better wait? We just got up from the breakfast table,' he said.

'That was ages ago,' said Ana and she waved her hand the way she saw her Mother doing it.

Grandad laughed and narrowed his eyes.

He was waiting for her next question. He knew she wanted another story, and not just any story. But he could see she had her own plan so he waited, patiently.

'Good cookies?' she said, handing another one to Tommy.

'Hmmm,' said the boy, stuffing his mouth, 'I wove them. I wove you too, Ana,' then he took two more and left. 'Thank you,' he remembered.

'Very tasty,' said Grandad too.

'I made them,' said Ana, 'with Grandma and Mother; we made some on Sunday afternoon for Daddy to take with him to work. Dad called them Ana's Cookies.'

Grandad smiled.

'That's very thoughtful of you.'

'Grandad, I have been wondering,' said Ana and she looked him straight in the eyes. 'How did Joyful Trouble get his name in the first place? You know, Trouble?'

Grandad smiled and helped himself to

another cookie. They were good. Tasted like Grandma's ones, but with a twist.

'Hmm,' he began. 'Told you he was good friends with the sailors. That started long before he even became a seaman himself. He would simply follow us around everywhere.'

'Everywhere?'

'Everywhere!'

'In the beginning some of us, seamen, had been asked to take this big dog around Simon's Town for walks. You see, his owners were busy people, his boy away at school and the dog was bored at home, alone. Trouble was new to town and his owners, the little boy's parents, were too busy to walk him. And so, we did. When you are a sailor and are asked by a superior to do a task you obey and don't ask questions.'

'Were you not scared of him?'

'Oh, we were. Him being so big. So we started with short walks at first, happy to do our chore and be done with it. But then one of us had said, one day: 'I walked the dog as far as the Church today!' 'The next day another seaman said: 'I walked the dog as far as the docks today!' And that was the beginning of it. I guess that's how our four legged friend got to know the town so well - and us, seamen. And the more we walked him, the further we strolled, the more time we spend with him and the better we got to know him. And he, us. And day by day we were less afraid and even looking forward to our daily walks.'

'Then we realized that we weren't walking him anymore, but he was leading us.

'And then he began going on walks all

by himself, for now he knew all the streets and all the alleys and, best of all, the shop owners of Simon's Town, especially the fishmongers'.

'But mostly he liked to tail seamen, to follow them, while they were moving in and out of the naval base. Out we went, the Great Dane was after us. In the train we climbed, the dog would jump in. Even in the dockyards when we were doing our job, he was there.

'He just liked to be amongst us, to sit amongst us, even lie amongst us and nap. Especially the ones working on the HMS Neptune,' smiled the old man while looking around for Tommy.

He didn't need to for the little boy was noisy enough, playing in the stream.

177

'Was that your ship, Grandad?'

'Yes, it was the ship I was first appointed to and served on for almost two years. She was a beautiful light cruiser patrolling the South Atlantic seas in pursuit of German heavy cruisers. Our motto was 'Regnare est servire', 'To reign is to serve', meaning sailing the seas and ruling them for our country, but it also means learning to live the good life.

'What do you think is the good life, Ana?'

Ana looked around at the remains of their picnic, at the shade tree and the river running smoothly and joyfully, singing over the rocks, towards the birds singing in the trees and minding their own life and at Tommy, pocking between

178

rocks with a stick, his cheeks red, his hair pasted along his temples by trickles of sweat.

'I think this is the good life, Grandad. What is the good life?'

'You are right, Ana,' smiled the old man. 'The love of your family,' and he pointed towards the remains of their picnic basked packed by Grandma and then towards Tommy. 'Seeing and enjoying the simple things around us,' and he gestured towards the trees. 'And doing what feel right here,' he concluded pointing towards his chest, 'what feels right in our hearts. Being true to oneself.'

'And was working on the ship a good life?'

'We certainly tried to make it a good

179

life and Joyful Trouble, oh, he helped us a lot! When seamen work on a ship it is always busy work, heavy work. And to get on and off the ship they lay a plank of wood a little bit wider than... this,' and the old man kept his hands wide apart.

'But our Great Dane enjoyed being amongst his seamen so much, that he thought the best place for him to sit and wait for his busy friends to finish their duties was on the plank itself, on the piece of wood connecting the ship with the shore. And you can't blame him, for that was the middle of all the action, the only area on which everyone walked. Because that was the only connection between the ship and the shore!

'Now, that was a narrow plank and

our dog was a big dog. Therefore not much space was left for the sailors to walk up and down on their duties. Every time a sailor would have to board or disembark the ship, sometimes even carrying heavy loads, he would be forced to step over our four legged friend. But after a few jumps like this the seamen, no matter how fond they were of our dog, would mumble and complain about how much trouble the dog was giving them.

'I guess Trouble felt the need to be amongst us. He grew up a happy puppy, free to follow his boy dressed in bell bottom trousers. When he found himself lonely again there were the sailors who first took him out for walks and gave him company. Perhaps from all the people in the world Trouble picked the seamen with their noticeable uniforms to make his own.

'Trouble!' they exclaimed.

'You're such a trouble.'

;You troublesome mate.'

'And the name stuck!

'Except that lots of joy was also associated with our trouble-causing-friend. Even if he was just one, Trouble managed to give all of us attention and humans love that, love feeling that they matter, even if to only one dog.'

'I hope every army had a Joyful Trouble,' said Ana.

'Oh, that's for sure! I remember reading long after the war was over that an American battalion found an abandoned Yorkshire Terrier in the jungles of Africa. They took pity of him, so small that an artillerist' helmet was too big for him to sleep in, and they adopted him. They took him with, fed him, kept him safe and named him Smoky. The tiny dog saved many a soldier's lives with his keen hearing; he would warn them of incoming artillery shells. Once Smoky even pulled a telegraph wire through a pipe, thus saving building time and keeping the engineers safe at the same time.'

'How small was he, Grandad?'

Grandad put her hands together. 'This small, he could easily fit in your palms. Small, but might brave. Told you, dogs just want us to be happy. Then they are happy too.'

'Joyful Trouble,' said Ana to herself while watching Tommy throwing stones in the stream.

Surprisingly enough, his clothes were still dry. Smiling at Grandad Ana picked up a chicken leg from the basket. She held it up, waving it towards her little brother.

'Tommy, food!'

Chapter 11

Naughty? Who do you call naughty?

The sun had just gone past their heads, but it was cool by the stream, in the shade of the great tree. The picnic basket was almost empty and, as a result, Tommy was quiet, lying drowsily in Grandad's lap.

'Grandad, were soldiers allowed to pick up lost dogs and keep them?'

'I don't' know if there was a rule denying it. Sure is that the dogs needed the soldiers just as much as the soldiers needed the warmth of a dog's gaze upon them. It was a humanitarian gesture in troubled times.'

'What's a humanitarian?'

'I know,' offered Tommy, 'it's like a vegetarian, but it eats humans.'

'Not quite, Tommy, but thank you for trying to help. A humanitarian is someone caring, someone who does a good deed out of the goodness of his own heart.'

'Grandad, was he ever naughty, Joyful Trouble?' said Ana, looking at her brother's scratched knees.

'Child, Joyful Trouble was a sociable, active, loving dog, but once he became a seaman he had to live his life by human rules. The Royal Navy's Code of Conduct is written for people, and not for dogs.

186

Joyful Trouble wasn't naughty, but he did break some of these rules although entirely by accident and never on purpose,' smiled Grandad. 'You could say that his intentions were always benign.'

'What's benign?'

'I know, offered Tommy again, serene. Benign is what you are after you are eight.'

'Not quite so, Tommy. Benign means nonthreatening. Joyful Trouble's intentions were never meant to cause harm. And I am sure that he never knew he is being disobedient. Just think. He had once been allowed to walk around town or board trains, all on his own. But now, as a seaman, he had to report for duty and follow a schedule. Free time

187

was being given to him, he could not take it whenever he fancied. How would a dog understand that he has to say where he goes and that he's only allowed to go for walks at certain times?

'That's why humans often complained that Joyful Trouble would go AWOL, that's Absent Without Leave, and it is a big offence in the Navy.

'But other times, when not even we, seamen, his friends, knew where he was, well, Joyful Trouble was helping out a pilot friend of his a naval aviator or an airdale, how we called them!'

'A pilot?' said Ana with big eyes.

'I want to be a pilot,' whispered Tommy stretching his arms and running around making low rrr sounds in his throat. 'I am a plane, I am a plane. Rrr, rrr. Oh that tickles my tongue. Rrrrrrr, that's ticklish.' Then he stopped as soon as he began, watching something on the ground right under his big toe.

'Grandad, do dogs have skin?'

'Yes, of course. Underneath all that fur. Why you ask?'

'Because skin keeps people from throwing up when they look at you.'

Ana turned red in the face and she looked sideways, trying hard to mask her giggle.

'You are so observant, Tommy,' said Grandad. Then he went on with his story.

'Told you he was a friendly dog. Sometimes Trouble would go to Wingfield, quite a distance from the Naval

189

Base. That's where our pilots were located. And there he would swap his round, white and navy Royal Navy cap for the blue-grey peaked cap of the Royal Air Force and thus go up, up in a military airplane,' and now

'Grandad's voice dropped to a whisper. 'THAT was illegal!

'But Joyful Trouble had extremely good eyesight and he would therefore

help his pilot friend to spot enemy submarines off the South African West Coast! Doing a bit of spy work we could say.

'They would fly up together in a small plane called Fairy Fulmer and Joyful Trouble would bark whenever he would spot a submarine! As simple as that. Although his ability to spot submarines is quite difficult to explain.'

'Why is that, Grandad?'

'Because he was a dog and dogs can't see as far as humans can. But dogs can see much better than humans when an object moves or when an object is in low light. Their eyes allow them to.'

'Maybe it was his hearing, Grandad.'

'You think so?' smiled the old man.

191

'Could be, yes indeed. His hearing was much more sensitive that of a human, he could have heard the low frequency, rumbling noise of the submarine's engine even past the plane's noise. And maybe that, combines with a dog's acute ability of spotting moving objects at far distances was the secret to his submarine spotting success.'

'Woof, woof,' said Tommy softly.

'A seaman AND a pilot,' smiled Ana. 'What else he did?'

'Do you find it funny, child?' said Grandad.

Ana's face turned red. 'I do.'

'Well, it was sort of funny for humans but it was normal behaviour for a dog, only that humans failed to notice it. Now

192

our dog was a seaman, therefore he had his own Conduct Sheet and Navy Rules and Regulations to live by - or at least to be judged by. Quite a few times,' the story went on, 'and this would have been the times when I couldn't accompany Joyful Trouble in his goings-on as I had my own chores to see to or we just happened to have a Field Day declared, a day when we had to stay and clean the ship. And since he had no pockets he accidently travelled on the railways without his pass - again!'

'Oh, no! The Ticket Collector!'

'Indeed. It was like this. Joyful Trouble and his mates were aboard a train. They chatted and laughed and had a merry time. They had food and some money and a whole day away from the docks; a whole day of fun and togetherness lay ahead of them.

'Ahem,' someone coughed and a stern face measured them all.

'It was the Ticket Collector!

'Tickets or passes, pleeez, he said slowly, looking at our dog.

'The other seamen produce their passes, but Joyful Trouble, not having any pockets, had no pass with him.

'So the Ticket Collector curled the corners of his moustache and smiled, searching in his bag where he kept his book. The pen, that he kept tucked behind his ear.

'One seaman without pass,' he sighed taking out... a bone and presenting it to the dog with a flourished bow. 'Thank you for saving my mother,' he smiled.

'But things didn't went this easy for Joyful Trouble on his return to the naval base for he went AWOL again. For this offence Joyful Trouble was confined to the banks of Froggy Pond with all the lampposts removed. Not that darkness bothered him much for his eyesight was excellent. And do you know what he did while he was there?'

Ana nodded, concerned.

'He slept. But I suspect he did something else too for in the morning his breath ponged of fish and other pond odours.'

'Fish,' whispered Tommy asleep and licked his mouth.

195

'He ate raw fish, Grandad? How could he?'

'Well dogs, although they can taste sweet, sour, bitter, salty and savoury just like us, humans do, they are less bothered by the flavour of the food because to them it doesn't taste as strong as it does to us. And their taste is strongly influenced by smell. If they like the smell they are more likely to eat the food. For humans both smell and taste are equally important. Not so for dogs. That's why dogs can eat fish and not minding its stench because they probably like it very much. To them, a morsel of fish is a map of faraway places, interesting and intriguing.

'Another time Joyful Trouble fell asleep in the wrong bed. And not just any bed, that was the issue. We, seamen, didn't mind Trouble cuddling with us or even taking over our beds. we just went and took over his bed for the night.

'This time around he had fallen asleep in the Petty Officer's dormitory. And that was a big offence because, although a

197

Petty Officer is a rank just above that of the Able Seamen, it is a higher rank and in the navy like all over military, respect is due to all the higher ranks.

'The punishment awarded him was: 'deprived of bones for seven days.'

'Oh, no! Did he miss his bones?'

'I guess he did because this was one of the weeks when he got into a fight of his own.'

'He got into a fight? But I thought he didn't like fighting.'

'Well, this wasn't that much of a fight, more of a power struggle. You see, other ships had dogs as mascots, but mere mascots, not enrolled as seamen. And those dogs were males, just like Joyful Trouble. But there was only one dock to rule over and too many dogs. Even two dogs sharing one dock is one too many,' smiled Grandad.

'That's how dogs are, they need to know that a certain territory belongs to them. Joyful Trouble was like that, him being used to look after his people and such. Perhaps it was also something inherited from his ancestors, the wolfs. Dogs, just like wolfs, like to mark their territory to alert other of their presence. That territory is important to them because it contains food, shelter and water that are important for survival. So they feel the need to defend it. Yes, dogs are similar to the wolfs, their ancestors, much more than we dare to imagine.'

'How come?'

199

'For once, dogs guard their territory and their resources, their food source, just like wolfs do. Then, when a dog rolls about in the dirt until his fur has caught that bad odour he's just been sniffing, it is actually his way of telling his family, be it a dog family or a human one, that there is food available somewhere near. Wolfs do just that. When mother wolf finds a carcass in the forest she would eat some and then return to the den. Here, she would allow each wolf in the pack to smell the scent of meat on her fur so that they can follow that odour trail though the forest and find whatever is left from the meal - and have some too.

'And just like wolfs, dogs growl, howl and whimper. But dogs' heads are smaller than those of wolfs and dogs' teeth are smaller and more rounder, probably due to the different types of foods the two species eat, and of course, dogs are better at working alongside people and at reading our body language and understanding us.

'So, returning to our fish-eating dog, the week he was without bones, maybe because he felt bored, maybe hungry, he picked up a fight with the mascot of HMS Redoubt. And let's just say that our dog won.'

'Woof, woof,' echoed Tommy.

'But Joyful Trouble had his moments of glory too,' smiled Grandad.

'He did?'

'Of course.

201

'Because of his amazing doings, he soon became a local celebrity. And because of that he was often invited as a special guest to local celebrations or fund-raising events. Of course, if he couldn't attend, a letter of apology was always sent on his behalf and it was almost always written by the Commander-in-Chief himself.

'And, do you know, during the time Joyful Trouble served in the navy, the Royal Navy had received plenty of applications for service, simply because of this dog's presence amongst us.'

'Gravy, yummy,' stirred Tommy and he suddenly opened his eyes.

'I'm hungry, Grandad.'

And Ana sighed and Grandad smiled and they both packed up the picnic basket and the blanket and headed back to the house, following Tommy who was running ahead, singing at the top of his voice:

'Gravy, gravy, in the navy.

Chapter 12

Good bye, Joyful Trouble

It took a whole day of waiting to hear the end of the story. It was a windy day and Tommy was trying his hand at flying a kite.

They were on the hill and Grandad was holding the kite's string. Right in front of him, his feet firmly pushed into the ground, his chin up and his eyes fiery with joy, was Tommy, holding onto the string too.

'Let me fly it, Grandad! Let me fly!' he

was shouting while pushing his back into the old man, trying to push him out of the way.

'This is a big kite, Tommy. It will take you flying up into the air. Better let me hold too. I'll only use one hand,' said Grandad.

'Promise?' sighed Tommy.

'Promise,' said Grandad while twisting the string of the kite firmly around his right hand. 'I'll put my left hand into my pocket. Hold on tight, you're in charge now.'

'My flying kite,' said Tommy, showing off all of his teeth. 'He is so tall, Grandad. Look, he flies with the clouds. No fear.'

Ana came to stand near Grandad.

She had a wishful look on her face and he knew just what it was.

'Joyful Trouble was a lot like this kite, you know?' said Grandad.

'Like a kite?' Said Ana and looked up

at the fierce piece of paper fighting the wind.

'I guess it does look like a dog,' she said, not very sure of the resemblance. 'At least they both have long tails.'

'In spirit, child,' said Grandad and smiled. 'I guess in tail too.'

Ana looked up at the kite, flying against a blue sky; it looked free and happy.

'Joyful Trouble had led a happy life most of the time,' began Grandad. 'Until one day, one day when he met a lovely Great Dane Lady. After that fatal encounter he's never been the same dog.'

'Fatal?'

207

'Yes, because he was incurably in love. Tail tucked in and ears pushed back, eyes narrowed, he wouldn't eat, he wasn't interested in his seamen friends, he didn't want to go in train rides; even the bones were left untouched.

'The Commander-in-Chief became worried, just like us, and he called a veterinarian to please come check our beloved dog. The vet couldn't find anything wrong, but upon asking the right questions about Joyful Trouble's whereabouts word came of him having met Adinda. And all became clear.

'Adinda?'

'Oh, yes, a lovely Great Dane Lady that Joyful Trouble met during one of his neighbourhood patrols.

'So the Commander made contact with Adinda's owners who, apparently, have met Joyful Trouble quite a few times and were familiar with his reputation. After bringing the two dogs together one more time, it was clear to everybody that our Joyful Trouble had met his match.

'It was the Commander himself who married the two dogs in love and many seamen shed a tear, believe it or not.'

'You too, Grandad?'

'Me too, child, me too. I was very happy for Trouble, for the joy in his heart. For what is a lonely life?'

'My kite, my kite,' sang Tommy, 'let it go, Grandad, let me fly it. Please and thank you!'

'Joyful Trouble was very happy now and we, the men of the seven seas, were happy with him, for him. He even led a family life, for he and Adinda had five puppies together.

'Of course, he was still a seaman and he still had to spend most of his time on the docks. But he would often receive leave to visit his family. I used to go with him, whenever I had time. Oh, he was such a good daddy!

'If one of the pups would come near him he would stand still and make sure he doesn't step on him by mistake. And if the pups would just walk underneath while he was standing, he would lift a paw at a time and hold it up until the pup was gone. So he won't step on one of his offspring by mistake.

'Sometimes, when the pups grew bigger and they became playful, he would let them to pull his ears or climb over his

211

body. He wouldn't in the least mind their sharp teeth or boisterous ways.

'Other times Adinda's owners told us how, during his visits, Joyful Trouble would feed his pups. Apparently they were very fond of apples and, quite by chance, there was a basket of apples on the kitchen table. Now, the puppies couldn't reach it, but Trouble could. He would carefully stretch his neck over the table, pick up an apple in his mouth and bite it once, enough to brake it in piece for his pups to enjoy.

'Other times the pups would start a fight over some toy. The first pup would have a toy and the second one would want it. So the second pup would run to

Trouble and begin playing with him until the first pup would drop the toy and come running to play along. At this moment the second pup would leave Trouble and go running to retrieve the most desired toy. At this, Joyful Trouble would stand, walk after the second pup and take the toy away, placing it on a table, out of sight.

'Other times, as the pups grew older, they began chewing house sleepers. But they were clever enough to cover their tracks. As soon as one of Adinda's owners would walk into the room, they would run and hide the chewed sleeper behind the sofa. Of course, Trouble found them and he picked up all the chewed sleepers placing them...'

213

'On the table?' asked Ana while tears of joy were rolling down her cheeks.

'Indeed. But one day, just like this kite flies with the wind then falls only to soar again, Joyful Trouble jumped off a truck and, miscalculating his distance, injured his leg - it was broken.'

'Oh, no!' said Ana, hands over her mouth.

'Accidents happen, child,' said Grandad slowly. 'That's why they are called accidents; because we can't foresee them. Best we can do is to take them as they come and make the most of it.'

'Joyful Trouble was like a kite,' said Ana softly.

'He was six and a half years old. That's when a Great Dane starts to be considered like a Grandad.

'It had been raining that week and the roads were wet and slippery. Joyful Trouble was riding in the back of a truck; he was returning from a visit to his family. After he jumped he skid on the wet stones, fell and broke a leg.

'The Commander-in-Chief saw to it that he received the best possible treatment, but due to his old age and the nature of the fall Joyful Trouble didn't quite recover. He couldn't walk anymore.

'So on Monday, 1 January 1944 he had been discharged from the Navy and went to live with Adinda and her human

215

family. His seamen friends never forgot him and he was receiving many visits, all the time.

'And just like the kite flies in the wind and tries to break free, so did Joyful Trouble decided one day that he will break free from his sore body. And so he did, on his seventh birthday, in 1944. It was his time.

'He had been born on Thursday 1 April 1937 in Rondebosch and had served in the Royal Navy for five glorious years, between 1939 and 1944.

'Joyful Trouble had been a friend to many and a great help too. With his gentle and loving nature and his long-life devotion he had been boosting the moral of many seamen stationed in the South Atlantic and fighting in the Second World War, and was never forgotten.

'His seamen friends remembered him as one of them, a bluejacket, a friend in need and great fun to be around, a free spirit.

'The Commander-in-Chief remembered him as an one of a kind Able Seamen, dependable and trustworthy, even though he was a for legged creature.

'The Ticket Collector remembered him as a true helper with extraordinary hearing abilities, one that could teach humans a lesson or two about empathy.

'His Royal Air Force comrades

217

remembered him as a dependable dog with an extraordinary sense of hearing and eyesight.

'And the people of Simon's Town remembered him as a saviour of the weak, defender of the needy and a big fan of titbits, always.

'And you, Grandad?'

'I will always carry Joyful Trouble's memory in my heart, tucked away with other fond memories. He gave me so much, without asking for much in return. He gave me hope and laughter and taught me that a day lived well is all that life is about. Joyful Trouble is the reason why I became so interested in dogs and enjoyed learning about them all my life.

'The day following his passing, the Royal Navy gave him a burial with full military honours and that day special

219

permission had been given to any seamen who wanted to attend. And they came in hundreds.

'Joyful Trouble was buried at Klaver Camp, on top of Red Hill, overlooking Simon's Town; the place he knew and loved so much. And his grave looks up at the blue sky, for now his spirit is as free as a kite.

'It was a special day for everyone, civilians, Royal Navy, the Air Force and even the Railway. Joyful Trouble's body was covered with a white Royal Naval Flag and a group of Royal Marines, his best friends, fired their weapons in his honour. Even a bugler was present, calling the 'Taps', a gentle, yet sad and lonely tune special for such occasions.'

The old man stretched his left arm towards the little girl.

'Come here, child,' and he hugged her close. Then standing tall and straight, his eyes towards the kite and the sky above, he sang softly:

'Day is done, gone the sun,

From the lake, from the hills, from the sky;

All is well, safely rest, God is nigh.'

Ana hugged her Grandfather.

'You loved him, Grandad?'

'Yes, I did.'

'I love you, Grandad.'

'I love you too.'

'Grandma's stew is made with love,'

221

said Tommy, hugging Ana. 'I'm hungry,' he added, dropping the cord of the kite and heading for the house.

Grandad was still holding the end of the string; Ana was holding Grandad.

'Should we let go?' said the old man softly.

'Yes,' smiled Ana, 'let it fly.'

222

'Free, just like Joyful Trouble,' whispered Grandad

'Happy,' said Ana, watching the kite enjoying the wind and its long tail flying on its own, disappearing out of view.

Forever and Ever

'Where to?' said the boy.

The puppy looked up then bounced ahead.

The day was warm, the sun was up and the country road stretched far ahead.

'Together?' said the boy and the puppy licked his hand.

'You and I, Boy, you and I,' said the boy and he skipped ahead on the dusty road.

The puppy followed and the puppy's tail wagged, as the boy sang.

And the dog's tail looked just like a kite's.

'You and I, Boy, you and I.'

The End

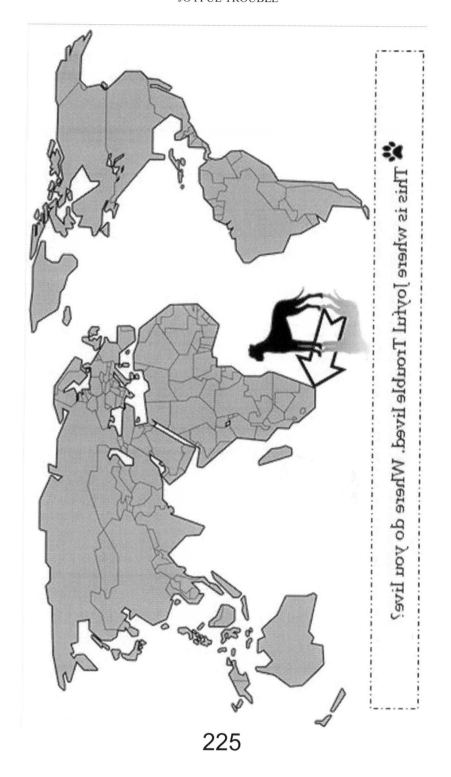

This is where Joyful Trouble lived. Where do you live?

Vetkoek Recipe

Vetkoek (read: fet-kuk) is a traditional South African fried dough bread common and much loved in Afrikaner cuisine.

It makes a tasty winter dinner or snack, served filled with cooked mince (ground beef) or with syrup, honey, or jam and grated cheese.

They're a great party snack if they are made small and filled with various processed meats, tuna and mayo, syrup, curried minced meat, cheese, or basically anything you feel like.

It originates from the traditional Dutch food, which date from the time of the migration period.

In the Caribbean, it is called "Johnny cake". It is similar in taste to Mexican sopapillas.

The word "vetkoek" literally means "fat cake" in Afrikaans or "fat cookie" in Dutch. It is similar in shape to a doughnut without a hole, and is made from flour, salt and yeast.

Ingredients

2 cups lukewarm water

1/4 cup white sugar

1 (or 0.25 ounce) package active dry yeast

7 cups all-purpose flour

afétéتة Tanز;

Iطن

2 teaspoons salt

3 cups oil for frying

Cooking Directions

Mix lukewarm water, sugar, and yeast in a small bowl. Let stand until yeast softens and begins to bubble slightly, about 5 minutes.

Sift flour and salt together in a large bowl.

Pour water mixture over flour mixture and knead until dough is smooth and elastic, 5 to 7 minutes. Cover bowl with clean cloth and let dough rise until doubled in volume, about 45 minutes.

Pinch off a piece of dough about the size of a tennis ball; roll until smooth.

Flatten ball of dough until it is the size of palm; set aside on a floured work surface. Repeat with remaining dough.

Heat oil in a deep-fryer or large saucepan to 350 degrees F (175 degrees C).

Fry flattened pieces of dough in the hot oil, 2 to 3 pieces at a time, until golden brown, about 3 minutes per side.

Cook's Note:

As you knead the dough, you may need to add more flour or water to get a dough the consistency of bread dough.

Parchment can be used for easier cleanup/removal from the pan.

Ana's Cookies Recipe

Ingredients:

2 eggs

2 cups of sugar

2 cups of oil

4 cups of flour

5ml Vanilla sugar OR 10ml lemon grind and 10ml lemon juice OR 5ml cinnamon

Icing sugar to dust on top when done (optional)

Cooking Directions

Beat the eggs well.

Add the sugar bit by bit, continuing mixing.

Add the oil and keep on mixing.

Add the desired spices.

Add the flour through a sieve and mix well.

To check if you have the right consistency for the dough, take some on a teaspoon and turn it upside down. If it stays, you are done. If it runs, you need to add more flour.

Use two teaspoons to help you place small, equal amounts in an oven pan. You do NOT need to spray the pan. Leave space between them as they will spread

Place the pan in a preheated over at 140C.

The cookies are done when they turn golden around the edges, 10 min the most.

Careful, they can burn easily - but they are still tasty.

Let them cool down before dusting with icing sugar.

Store in an air tight container lined with paper towels for up to two weeks, if no one finishes them.

Sneak Peek

As Good as Gold,
a dog's life in poems

WHY, HEDGEHOG?

Just over the meadow, just over the hill,

Where the grass is greener and the stream runs slow,

There's a spot that many walk past and few really know.

Here's where puppy likes to go and explore.

He came here today,

He's here right now.

Oh, puppy,

Watch out!

Just over the meadow, were the trees grow tall

And the shade is thick and the grass is soft,

Puppy rolls all over then he lies dead, sloshed.

This is his kingdom; he's the King, the servant and the fool...

But something's new in the grass today...

Ouch!

It pricked his nose

And his behind.

Just over the meadow and right down the hill

A puppy yelps and licks his snout; something's amiss!

His Kingdom's been invaded, time for attack!

The growl troops are summoned while the tail's tugged for retreat…

Puppy tiptoes,

Takes a peek.

Sniffs carefully….

What IS that squeak?

Just over the meadow, hidden in the green, lush grass,

A creature as small as a… ball wanders about.

Not quite round, with pointy nose and… needles, no doubt!

"What is the use of those?" barks puppy from afar.

Two beady eyes
Smile at pup.
"What is the use of a tail?"
The creature asks.

Just over the meadow, right down the hill,

A puppy and a hedgehog sit together, two chums.

And chat of this and laugh at that, mostly insects and bugs,

Then they both roll around, each one on his meadow half.

For a Kingdom at war is of use to none.

Better share and make friends with your strange neighbour,

Enjoy together a snack, there are plenty about

And share the shade, lots of it to go around.

RAIN, A HAIKU

Drip-drip, plop-plop, rain,

Making grass grow taller.

Breakfast for friend snail

Jock of the Bushveld
Africa's Best Loved Dog Hero

In the heart of South Africa it is said

That once upon a time lived a brave

dog: Jock of the Bushveld.

His owner took down his stories

Of love, respect and glory;

And adventures, uncounted.

For Jock was one of a kind, his

bravery by very few exceeded.

The runt of the litter, the smallest of

puppies,

The last one to eat, yet first to be

picked on,

238

Jock was a bull terrier not tall, yet not short either

Not at all like his brothers: none liked the poor mongrel.

"I'll have him!" said a loving man at once,

"Everyone deserves a fair chance."

Jock showed good nature and a big heart,

Good eyesight and a rather forte bark.

His fur, golden with chocolate strikes,

God's sign that he was precious;

His ears, always cocked

For he was always listening.

The Cheetah and the dog

Two wet noses met one day,

Quite by chance, each one on a trail.

The sun was high, the day was hot,

When dust blew up you could see not.

Such are Africa's wild plains,

With long, hot summers and tails with tales.

About the Author

Patricia Furstenberg came to writing though reading, after finishing her medical degree, her passion for books being something she inherited from her parents.

She loves to write stories and poems about amazing animals. She believes each creature has a story and a voice, if only we stop to listen.

Patricia is passionate about literature, mind, brain education and culture in general and she often writes on this topic for The Huffington Post South Africa. She also has her own blog, Alluring Creations, http://alluringcreations.co.za/wp/

Patricia won the Write Your Own Christie Competition. The Judges, Mathew Prichard, David Brawn from Harper Collins UK and Daniel Mallory from Harper Collins US "were impressed by her thorough investigation and admired the strength of her narrative."

When she's not writing Patricia likes to read, read, read, drink coffee, listen to music and connect with her readers.

One of the characters portrayed in her children's story "Happy Friends" is Pete, the yellow toy elephant. Not many know, but Pete exists and lives in Pat's home.

Patricia lives happily with her husband, children and dogs in sunny South Africa.

242

Made in the USA
Middletown, DE
03 August 2019